Praise for STARS LIKE ACID

"*Stars Like Acid* is an emotionally resonant work that carves out an intriguing niche within the genre." ~BOOKLIFE by PUBLISHERS WEEKLY

"Stars like Acid blew me away and definitely has me perusing new shelves at the library! With twists and turns throughout, SLA will keep you flipping the pages well into the night. This book charges the emotions, sparkles with love and overcoming obstacles." ~RONICA, Goodreads Reviewer

"I loved this book! It has the best of everything, sci-fi, romance, and a little fantasy. The characters are easy to relate to and fall in love with, and the writing is beautiful." ~AMANDA STUNTZ, Author of Witch's War

"With explorations of oppressive government oversight, out-of-control human evolution, and humanity adapting to life beyond Earth, *Stars Like Acid* calls to mind complex space sagas like *The Expanse*." ~DANIEL ROMAN, Winter is Coming dot net

"I loved Tea & Annabelle we get dual pov so we can have a better view of everything! There are twist and turns through the story and also the writing is compelling!" ~Readmore Sleepless blog

"Marissa created an amazing story with a unique premise, loads of twists and turns, and plenty of diverse characters to root for along the way!" ~NIKKI, Besties Write Stuff blog

"This book was incredibly emotional, and Rissa isn't scared to show us the good, but especially the horrors that could happen in a dystopian society. I couldn't put this book down..." ~AMBER CROOK, Goodreads Reviewer

Also By Marissa Lupe

Book One:
STARS LIKE ACID

Stars Like Fire

Book Two of the Stars Like Acid series

Marissa Lupe

Howlite Publishing LLC

Howlite Publishing LLC
Meeker, CO
United States
marissalupe.com
Stars Like Fire

First Edition, 2024
This is a work of fiction. Names, characters, business, events, and incidents
are the products of the author's imagination. Any resemblance to actual
persons, living or dead, or actual events is purely coincidental.
eBook ISBN: 978-1-960824-03-5

Paperbook ISBN: 978-1-960824-04-2

Hardback ISBN: 978-1-960824-05-9

Library of Congress Control Number: 2024900952

Fiction/Science Fiction/General

Formatting interior book design and cover art by

Howlite Publishing LLC

For my boys...

Note to readers...

This novel includes difficult subject matter showing the aftermath of child abuse, medical experimentation, torture, thoughts of suicide, murder, and death.

Contents

Prologue

S pace

Annabelle

When she awoke, she knew something was different. She felt weightless and could see nothing but darkness.

She tried to speak. "Hello?" But no sound came. It was as though her thoughts echoed out into nothingness.

She looked down, and fear gripped her insides, but she had no insides. Annabelle saw that she had no body. Her reaction was to hyperventilate, but without a body, it was as if her mind began folding in on itself, and just as she was about to descend into madness, she heard a voice.

"It's okay." The voice was small but kind.

"Who's there? What's happening to me?" Annabelle asked.

"I know this is a lot to process, but you're dead." The voice was full of sadness and hesitation like someone who didn't completely know how to handle things of this magnitude.

Terror unspooled like a giant white ribbon floating through space. Annabelle tried and failed to grab onto something.

The voice rose in pitch and desperation. "Try giving yourself a body, that helps sometimes."

"And how am I supposed to do that?" Her mind shouted.

"Just see yourself. You knew what you looked like. Picture yourself standing in front of you, then put your consciousness into it." The voice made it sound so easy, so simple.

How the fuck am I supposed to do that?

But with no other options, she gave it a try. Starting with her feet, she pictured one toe at a time, and suddenly, there before her, a ghostly toe wiggled at her.

An uncomfortable laugh escaped Annabelle and she kept going. Legs, torso, arms, neck, head, face, hair. Hovering like a see-through shell, was a copy of Annabelle. Annabelle laughed, and her copy laughed causing shockwaves to crash through her, the copy's eyes widened. Then it smiled. She had always wanted to explore Earth, specifically Australia, with its adorable fluffy, gray-faced koala bears with their large black oval noses. When the copy's head became a koala head, Annabelle laughed, and when the koala laughed an eerie feeling came over her.

Nope. This is too weird.

The copy returned to normal. She tried not to think of the impossibility of it all and focused. She thought of herself, her consciousness, as a ball of light and floated into the ghost-Annabelle.

She opened her eyes.

Looking down this time, she saw her transparent fingers flex, but it was a strange disconnect to not feel the tendons, muscle, or flesh. To only see the fingers move through sheer will was strangely God-like, she was a puppet master. Annabelle looked around but still saw nothing.

"Where are we?" she asked.

"The in-between." the small voice said.

"Are you God?"

The small voice laughed, and for the first time, Annabelle recognized it as the voice of a child, a boy. But with the most unique accent she had ever heard, she couldn't place it even though she had thorough lessons on the various continents on Earth while growing up.

He laughed again. "You're funny."

Annabelle was about to ask what was so funny about her question when the boy spoke again. "I'm not supposed to be here. I could get in a lot of trouble for helping you. So, I have to go soon."

Panic threatened to overtake Annabelle. She could not be left alone in this darkness.

"It's okay, there will be others." He said. "You can show them the way. Like I'm going to show you."

Fear twirled within Annabelle. "Wait! How can I follow you if I can't see you?"

"Just think of my voice like a vine."

Annabelle did as she was told, and suddenly a vine, long, thick, and green with thorns, appeared out of nowhere.

"Now grab hold." The boy said.

As soon as Annabelle touched the vine, she was sped through the cosmos. Planet after planet raced past her almost too quickly to see, and the stars streamed by her so fast it was as if they were white shining rivers weaving their way around her.

Then just as suddenly as it had started, it stopped. Annabelle looked down and saw the most beautiful planet she had ever seen.

The boys' voice came again. "This is where you'll take them."

"Wait. Take who?"

"The others. It's starting now. The souls are looking for their matches, for their families. You can show them." The small voice started drifting away.

"Wait, don't go!" Annabelle twisted her ghostly hands, trying to push down the small bubble of panic within her. In a small voice she said. "I don't want to be alone."

The boys' voice softened but was still hurried. "It's okay now. Just think of Earth and you'll be there. It'll all make sense soon. Promise."

Desperation clawed through Annabelle. "Please, stay with me."

"I'm sorry, I must go. But don't worry, you'll save them."

"Wait. Save who? From What? Hello?"

The loneliness and fear were overwhelming. Annabelle started to feel her ghost form unravel. She forced herself to envision her body, whole, and calm. It worked; her ghostly body formed back to complete.

With no other options, she decided to trust the boy. She pictured Earth and suddenly, she was there. This time she wasn't floating in nothingness, but in the familiar comfort of the stars. The view she had grown up watching.

The idea of traveling the galaxy without limitations started to have its appeal. For the first time since she had awakened, hope began to grow. She thought of the rings of Saturn, and just as she was going to transport there, she heard a new voice. This one, much older, and female.

"Hello? Is anyone there?"

The voice was fearful, and Annabelle smiled knowing now that she could make a difference for all the lost souls.

Annabelle calmly replied. "It's okay, I'm here, I can help you." And a smile formed on her lips.

Chapter One

Eleanor

Five Years Ago

Dust motes circled the air in a stream of sunlight as Eleanor teetered on the edge of a worn wooden stool. The frayed rope around her neck scratched her skin. She tucked her fingers underneath the rope and moved it side to side trying to find a more comfortable position. *How ironic*, she thought. Looking for comfort when she was about to end it all.

The abandoned attic was as good a place as any to make her departure. Surrounded by the remnants of her family things, packed up in boxes and long ago hidden away. She had come to the decision three days ago, a quick moment really, when she realized Zephyr no longer needed her. After the General had taken everything, her home, her family, her freedom, the young boy was her only reason for living. Eleanor saw how cruel the General was to his son, and Zephyr had no one else in his corner after his mother had died.

So, she lived.

For him.

But he was grown now. Stronger than her, taller than her, more resilient and capable than her. He didn't need Eleanor anymore, and without freedom, without a way to live her own life, doomed to fulfill every cruel order the General demanded, what was the point of living at all?

An unnatural calm washed over her as she took one final breath and stepped off the stool.

A sharp hard tug brought a rush of blood to her brain. She instantly regretted the decision. She struggled, but only for a moment before the rope snapped and she fell hard to the ground with unfettered relief. Her neck burned where the rope had dug in, and her right hip had landed on something sharp, but she welcomed the pain, it was a reminder that she was still alive. No matter how trying it may be, life was always a gift to be grateful for. She lay there breathing heavily, until she curled into a ball, hugging herself, then Eleanor cried.

The last rays of sunlight had gone, and the attic was bathed in darkness by the time her tears stopped, leaving crusty rivets on her cheeks. She slowly unfurled herself, muscles aching, and body cold. As she shakily got to her feet, she knocked over a stack of boxes, and inside one, she spotted something that sent a thrill through her.

A laptop.

Information was under complete control of Dunamis, and technology like cell phones and laptops were mostly reserved for the higher elite. It had been years since Eleanor had access to anything beyond Sandstone Estate gossip.

But if this laptop was the one she thought it was, the owner-her deceased sister in law, was no ordinary person. It would already be connected to a secure network as long as the General hadn't discovered and shut it down, which she highly doubted. He would have had to know about the network in the first place in order to shut it down.

Her heart raced as she dug it out of the box and hastily opened it up. She held the power button down, but her heart sank when nothing happened. She dug further into the box and tried to contain her excitement when her hand wrapped around a power cord. She searched for an outlet but could hardly see by the faint moonlight. She finally spotted one next to the light switch by the door.

She hurriedly weaved around the stacks of boxes, unraveled the cord, and plugged the laptop in. After a few agonizing seconds the bright screen lit up, along with her heart and her smile. The laptop was an older model with no fingerprint recognition, only a passcode, which Eleanor knew by heart after all her years assisting her sister-in-law.

Her fingers soared along the keys tapping in the passcode, and a pleasant chime rang out to her ears when the welcome screen opened. Long ago, before Eleanor was the President's aide, she was a librarian. Eleanor used this laptop more than her sister-in-law, and there, in the corner of the screen, was the familiar logo for an app that librarians utilized to chat with each other. She quickly opened it up and laughed with pure joy when she saw thousands of old notifications waiting for her.

In that moment, it felt as if Eleanor had a small corner of her life back.

She had the most powerful thing in the world... Eleanor, had hope. Hope for a life of her own again someday.

Over the next few months Eleanor would sneak off to the attic when the rest of the estate was asleep, and she would read. Post after post, comment after comment. Flying through as much information as she could absorb. She didn't risk posting or opening any other apps for fear of alerting anyone to her newfound access. But she would watch, and she would read, and after not too long Eleanor discovered a faction of resistance operating on the librarian chat app.

A specific chat room labeled "Quintessential Novels" was clearly using coded language. Not so clear to the untrained eye, but to Eleanor, the members of the "Quintessential Novels" chat group were relaying information right under the nose of Dunamis.

The 'Classics' meant they were speaking of a time before The Decline. 'Bestsellers' insinuated talk about high-ranking Dunamis officials. And 'Fantasy" meant the discussion was about individuals who possessed a Connex gene and had managed to escape the reach of Dunamis gene testing.

This chat room is where Eleanor met Mabel.

Mabel inspired Eleanor to be brave. Her courageous tales of helping Connex gene carriers across borders and moving banned books to safe houses inspired Eleanor to finally participate in the chat. No longer an observer, but a contributor, Eleanor bonded with Mabel.

Before long, the two had established a routine. Every Tuesday and Thursday after the rest of the staff had gone to sleep, Eleanor and Mabel chatted. Her heart raced all day leading up to their chat time. The one bright light within her existence of darkness, Mabel became Eleanor's entire world. For years their chats gave Eleanor something to look forward to, a reason to live. Their conversations grew more intimate over time. Then, they began video-chatting, and the moment Eleanor first saw Mabel's dark brown soulful eyes she knew that she was in love with this woman.

Present Day

It had been nearly a year since Téa had destroyed the satellites and internet and cellular phones went down. Every day without Mabel was a day masked with pain for Eleanor. When news of the General's defeat reached Eleanor, her immediate thought was of Mabel's safety. Eleanor was aware there were loyalists trying to weed out people who had, in their minds, betrayed Dunamis. Eleanor had a vague idea of where Mabel was living, somewhere along the East coast between what used to be Delaware and

Maryland. But she had no way to know for certain, and no way to reach her.

But recently hope began to take root again in Eleanor's heart, because Téa, with help from the resistance, had brought back radio communication to Sandstone. More than ever, Eleanor wanted to share with Mabel all the new and wonderful things in her life. How it felt to be rid of the General, their progress in restoring an independent nation, and most of all, her newfound family.

Every night for the past few weeks after Téa had fallen asleep, Eleanor went to the CB radio and tried to find Mabel channel by channel. She knew it was a long shot, Mabel would've had to have her own shortwave radio, but it was all Eleanor could do. It was her only hope.

After weeks of disappointment, Eleanor finally decided to confide in Téa in the chance her niece would give her a vehicle, some gas, and encourage her to go find Mabel.

It was Celia's four-week-old milestone and Téa was documenting the occasion with a mini photoshoot in the morning sun.

Eleanor caught her eye and Téa said. "Hey Auntie, Ian and his family are going to come to visit the week after next to meet Celia. Do you mind helping me get a guest room ready?"

Eleanor was quiet, deep in thought. If Ian and his family were here, Eleanor would not feel so guilty about leaving her niece for a short while. "Of course darling, how long are they staying?"

"About a week I think, Emma is fairly far in her pregnancy, so I don't think they want to stay too long. The Sanctuary has an excellent obstetrician that they won't want to be away from for long."

Eleanor's blood rushed through her veins, a smile curving her lips, a whole week to search for Mabel without feeling like she was leaving her niece alone. "Téa dear, I wonder..." How could she tell her niece she wanted to leave and find a woman she had never met? Then the idea came to her. "You mentioned hitting a snag with the telephone installation along the eastern coastline. I wonder if, since you'll have the company, you might want me to assist with that and take a trip to the coast for the week they are here?"

Téa tilted her head and narrowed her eyes in her direction. As if she was staring intently at her, no doubt taking in the fine lines around Eleanors hazel eyes, and dark hair wrapped up in her daily elegant bun. "Auntie, you have never shown interest in getting involved in the rehabilitation process or any Dunamis outreach at all... Why now?"

Eleanor twisted her hands in her lap, then slowly stood, taking Téa's hands in her own, and looked her niece in the eye. "I have not been completely forthcoming with you dear." Eleanor gulped, took a deep breath, and continued. "I had a friend, from before we lost the satellites, that I would speak with on a regular basis. We became close, and I think of her often. I would like to try to find her."

Téa grinned widely at her and gripped her hands tighter. "Auntie! Why didn't you tell me sooner? I could have helped, of course, go find your *friend*." Téa said with a wink.

Eleanor blushed and Téa continued speaking. "Don't worry about the telephone installation, you just go and find... What's her name?"

Eleanor relaxed her hands and pulled her niece to her side, whispering. "Mabel, her name is Mabel, and I do miss her terribly."

"Well, you take all the time you need, don't worry about me and Celia, if it takes you longer than a week, Angie and William will still be here, we won't be alone."

Eleanor shook her head. "No my darling, I will not leave you, I'll be back by the time Ian and his family have finished their visit, one week, and I'll be back."

Téa smiled and pulled her into an embrace. "I hope you find her, Auntie."

"Me too darling, me too."

Chapter Two

Theo

T he sun beat down, an unrelenting force set on scorching away any and all source of relief from the elements. No shade. Not even a breeze.

Theo tried to protect himself as best he could with a rag soaked in water that hung around his strong shoulders, burnt and blistered from the long days working outside. His muscular lean frame rippled with each movement as he dug his hands into the earth. Soil permanently colored the underside of his fingertips, no matter how short he clipped his nails, or how long he scrubbed his hands, the stain remained.

His clear gray eyes squinted at the flaming rays of sun trying to overtake the view of the expansive fields.

Ever so delicately Theo laid the seeds in a line and covered them with a thin layer of dirt. Row after row Theo worked under the sun. The farmland stretched on for yards, as far as the eye could see. In a few weeks' time, little green sprouts would shoot from the ground, his reward for a job well done.

He took a deep sigh of relief at the sound of the lunch bell ringing out over the land. He rose from his knees and dusted his hands off on his tan coveralls, the white sleeveless shirt underneath stained a light yellow from overuse. His next purchase with his minimal pay would be a new thin long sleeve shirt to protect his arms, after that a hat; oh, what he wouldn't give for a hat.

Theo made his way to the two-story farmhouse with peeling paint, that had a large wrap-around front porch where Gertrude, a pale middle-aged stout woman with dark blue eyes, had prepared lunch.

Theo smiled. "What are we having today, Gertrude?" When she didn't answer, Theo grinned and continued. "Let me guess, I bet it's a thick slice of steak topped with garlic herb butter, served with carrots and potatoes, am I right?" He asked with a wink.

Gertrude, with her greying curly hair wound tightly in a bun, threw Theo a glare and shook her head. "Boy this ain't no fancy five-star joint, you get what you get, and you'll be grateful for it!" She scooped a ladle full of brown runny mush and sloshed it into a bowl. She shoved it at him and handed him a slice of bread.

Theo gave her a half bow and grinned. "Wonderful as always Gertrude, best chef this country has ever seen."

Gertrude rolled her eyes and raised her ladle as though she were ready to swing it at him. Theo scurried away and threw some parting words over his shoulder. "Thank you, ma'am! I'll see you at dinner time!"

Theo ate his lunch with his fingers, scooping the mush up with his bread, he could be eating cardboard and still feel grateful for something to fill his hungry belly. He knew he should be grateful to have a job, and a room to sleep in at night, even if it was above the dusty old barn; and no matter how small the pay was. But he longed for something more, for answers about who he was.

He was the only hired hand on the farm. Gertrude, despite her rough exterior, and her husband Phil, were the kindest people Theo had ever met. As a mixed-race couple, Gertrude with her light skin and Phil with his dark skin, had lived their former lives as outcasts. Not that it was illegal, but during the General's rule, the sparse population of people of color had been looked down on. Phil, not wanting his son to face the discrimination he had, always told Theo it was a miracle their son came out looking exactly like his mother, and nothing like his father. Something about the sadness in Phil's eyes when he had said that, broke Theo's heart. But since the General's downfall, they no longer had to live in fear.

They wanted a better life for their child, so they joined the Dunamis rehabilitation program aimed at restoring the Midwest to its former glory. The program supplied seed, water cost reimbursement, and employee benefits in exchange for farming the land. The area was previously uninhabitable, but some miracle baby who could draw poison from the Earth had traveled through town, which, coupled with the growing positivity of a hopeful nation, provided the ability to make things grow again. Or so he was told by his employers and the social worker at the hospital. It all sounded crazy, and his brain told him that it all seemed too good to be true. But somewhere deep within him, he knew it was right. Something about it made sense and lined up with his heart, so he believed them.

Gertrude, Phil, and their son Elijah were the first family to sign up for the Midwest section of what was once North America. They were excited by the chance to build a better home for their family, and they were allowed to hire one farm hand, Theo. Through the program, the new Dunamis also paid their medical bills for Elijah's care.

Theo had been selected for employment during his stay in the hospital. He remembered that day months ago, when his doctor said they had found a place for him to go. He had been on the mend from his injuries, and the hospital had graciously allowed him to stay for a short while, hoping that a family member would come to claim him. But no one ever came. So, the hospital's social services officer started to help him find a place to stay. The best he could hope for was a halfway house. Then he lucked out when he was told they found him a job. That it would be hard manual labor, but it was his best option for someone with no known history.

Theo had a longing for something more, for family, for connection; but was relieved that he would have some-where to live. With no memory of how he arrived at the hospital, no recollection of his life at all, not even a name.

No one knew how he had come to be there in his condition; unconscious, a stitched-up bruising neck, and his scans showed signs of prior suffocation. Someone must have told the nurses his name during admittance, it had been on his wristband, Theo Jones.

Theo gingerly rubbed the ugly scar that ran across his throat. He was finishing the last bite of his lunch in his room. He sat on the moderately sized bed with a rusted metal frame and soft blue quilt, his legs kicked up onto a tiny bale of hay, when he heard a small yet clear voice. "Hey, Theo you up here?"

A smile formed on Theo's lips. "Yeah kid, up here!" He called out.

Elijah made his way up the barn steps very slowly. The heavy clacking of his elbow crutches sounded loudly with each careful step. A small tuft of dark copper frizzy hair popped up as Elijah finally made it to the top of the landing.

Theo hustled over to Elijah and without touching him hovered his hand behind the small boy's back just in case he should fall.

"You know kid, your mom doesn't like you climbing these stairs."

Elijah shrugged his shoulder away from Theo and tried to sound as gruff and grown-up as an eight-year-old could. "What mama don't know won't hurt her. Besides, I feel good today, Theo." He made his way to Theo's bed and sat down, setting his crutches to the side. He lifted one of his thin, pale, tired legs with his hands, just a little to cross it over his other, matching how Theo liked to sit with ankles crossed and limbs stretched out.

Theo chuckled under his breath and tousled Elijah's hair. "You've got spirit kid, your mama sure does scare me, you've got to be the bravest person I know to defy her."

Elijah laughed. "Ah, she ain't so bad, barks worse than her bite. Mama won't never really hurt me."

Theo grinned. "I suppose you're right. So, tell me, what happens next in 'Dr. Symbico vs. Sir Festivus'? I'm dying to know."

Elijah regaled Theo with fanciful descriptions of an epic battle between good and evil. Elijah was a big fan of comic books and looked forward to his weekly visits to the recently reopened town library. The boys had their meeting every time Elijah finished a new issue, although usually, they met on the porch. Elijah's condition made things like stairs a dangerous obstacle for his weak legs that could give out on him at any moment. Truthfully, Theo enjoyed his company, he was a cool kid, and it was a nice break from Theo's otherwise monotonous life.

When Elijah finished telling Theo his summary of the latest issue of his favorite comic series, Theo helped him back down the stairs, and then went back to work.

By the time the sun was setting, Theo's muscles ached, and his head felt like it was on fire. He went to the outdoor shower behind the barn. It was a five foot across barrel and five feet high with a swing-out door. A single shelf with a hook was attached to the back of the barn next to the shower, where he could place his soap and hang his towel. He stepped inside and pulled the curtain around him, undressed, and tossed his clothes to the ground. The cold water washed away the heat, dirt, and sweat.

After a quiet dinner inside the farmhouse with the family, of red beans and rice, Theo headed to his room. Sleep came fast and easy for Theo, dreamless and restful preparing to do it all again day after day.

The next morning Phil hollered at Theo from the front porch as he was about to head out to the fields. "Hey Theo, wait a minute, Son!"

Theo turned to face Phil who was tall, with close cropped hair, and jogged back towards the porch. "Yes, what do you need sir?"

Phil stood with his fists clenched on his hips and huffed. "Our water heater busted this morning; I've got quite the mess to clean up in the basement. Wondering if you can head to the hardware store for me and pick up the new one and some parts? Orders already been placed, Bill already knows you're heading that way for me, has it all ready for ya."

Theo nodded and took the truck keys that Phil held out for him. "Of course, sir, happy to help." Theo lazily saluted Phil as he left and jogged towards the truck.

Headed down the mostly empty highway towards town twelve miles away, Theo had the radio on full blast, playing an old cassette tape that was left in the truck, some old rock song. A tan hand draped out the window catching the air, a breeze sweeping through his light brown hair. He was singing at the top of his lungs, swaying his head side to side. "Cause I'm freeee! Like a bird now!"

He pounded his other hand on a knee mimicking a drum when he heard a small cry. Theo looked in the rear-view mirror and to the sides of the road but didn't see anything. He was about to sing some more when he heard it again.

"Help!"

Theo was sure he heard it that time. He turned the radio all the way down and listened intently.

"HELP! Theo, STOP!"

Theo slammed on the brakes and a loud thump sounded from behind him. He heard Elijah. "Ow, why'd ya slam the brakes so hard?"

Theo jumped out of the cab and hustled to the bed of the truck. Sure enough, a crumpled Elijah lay in the back covered by a tarp.

Panic seized Theo's chest. "Elijah! What the heck are you doing back there? Trying to get yourself killed?"

Elijah's voice was small, he peeked over the tarp, face timid. "I'm sorry Theo, I just wanted to go to town with you, but I knew Ma would never let me come."

Guilt grabbed Theo's voice. "I'm sorry I yelled kid; you just scared me is all." He reached for the boy and his crutches. "Come here, let me help you down, let's get you into the cab."

Elijah looked up, bright blue eyes watery. "Thanks Theo." He wiped his nose on his sleeves and reached for Theo to help him down.

Theo buckled Elijah into the passenger seat and kept driving. "Well, we're too far now to go back, we'll call Phil and Gertrude when we get to the hardware store."

Elijah smiled so big; it was as if happiness had taken over his whole body. Theo tousled the boy's hair. "No more joy rides though promise?"

Elijah held out his pinky towards Theo. "I promise."

Theo wrapped his own pinky around Elijah's, sealing their pact.

Chapter Three

Eleanor

It had been eight days since Eleanor had left Sandstone for the eastern coast. A depleted population had made her search easier. Instead of wading through full cities, she only had to go to the center of the few communities that were left. She visited every established town, and every abandoned village, with no luck. Eleanor was down to her last gas reserves and had just enough to make it back to Sandstone plus a dozen or so miles. Soon she would have to give up.

Eleanor was seated at an old table. She picked at the chips in the wood top as she contemplated her next move, the table wobbled when Eleanor placed her elbows on it. She could hear seagulls through the open glass window, the scent of saltwater wafted towards her as she sipped her drink. Goodness, how she missed the sound of birds and the feel of fresh ocean air on her skin.

More luxurious things such as eating out at restaurants were slowly returning as people grew their own food and no longer had to rely on Dunamis rations. Lucky for Eleanor, she was able to find home-run guest rooms to stay in during her travels, and home-run restaurants for places to eat.

This home was particularly small, and the furniture was old, from before The Decline. But the owner was kind and had made her stay comfortable.

She looked out of the small front bay window of the house diner, which was an average-sized living room cleared out and filled with three small tables and mismatched chairs. Eleanor blew on her hot chai tea latte and took another drink when she heard two men whispering at the table behind her. Their rough grating voices carried.

-"I heard the loyalists rounded up the rest of them last night. Being sent to the Cliffhouses."

- "Good. Selfish women, refusing to procreate, how will the population survive without the old Dunamis?"

- "Exactly, at least with the General you knew there would be a steady increase of people."

- "They say if you toss the guard a slice of fresh meat, he'll let you inside for one hour."

A gross smirking chuckle came from both men, and Eleanor's skin crawled.

- "Well then, perhaps I'll be slicing up our fish reserves, gotta do my civic duty."

Eleanor's blood ran cold, and her legs had gone numb. It couldn't be. She knew Mabel was no longer of prime reproduction age, like Eleanor, she was in her late fifties. Was this where *her* Mabel was? Eleanor had to be sure, she had to find these Cliffhouses, but who could she ask?

Eleanor waited until the men had gone. She had a pleasant conversation with the homeowner the night before, maybe it would be safe to ask.

She approached the homeowner, who was an elderly Latino gentleman currently wiping up the tables, he had introduced himself when she first arrived looking for a room to stay in. "Hey, Fred, those men who just left."

Fred stiffened and looked at Eleanor with fear in his dark eyes.

Eleanor continued cautiously. "They mentioned something about Cliffhouses."

"No, no I don't know nothin bout that." Fred shook his head as he walked away, he had a noticeable limp from multiple hip replacements.

Eleanor gently grabbed Fred by the elbow and spoke softly. "Fred please, I'm looking for a friend of mine, I won't tell anyone that you helped me, please, where are the Cliffhouses?"

Fred looked at Eleanor as though deciding if she could be trusted. Finally, he said. "The loyalists round up women who refuse to match up with a male mate. They fear the population will continue to decline if all women are not producing babies."

Fred paused and shook his head, dropped his eyes to his toes, a small hiccup came from the man, and when he looked back up his old eyes had welled up with tears. "They grabbed my granddaughter, Amber." He gripped the edge of a table for support. "Mi nieta es la luz de mi vida." He looked desperately at Eleanor. "My granddaughter is the light of my life. It's been only the pair of us since, mi hijo, her father passed away."

He paused again and his shoulders shook before he took a deep breath and steadied himself. "The loyalists tried to match her with a boy here in town, she refused. She told them that we were a free nation again and she did not love that boy." Fred wiped his wrinkled light brown hand with thick knuckles down his face. "The loyalists said she could have one month to find a boy to love." Fred pounded his fist on the tabletop. "Silly girl should have listened to them then, but she had kept talking, she shouted at them, that she would fall in love with the person and not their gender. That she was fluid with su amor." Fred's tears finally escaped him. "They dragged her away, kicking and screaming. They threatened to kill her if any single person intervened."

The old man grabbed Eleanor's forearms; his words came out desperate. "They will kill you Miss, and perhaps my granddaughter as well, you must stay away."

Eleanor placed her own hands on the man's forearms as well, a half embrace, took a deep breath and looked him dead in the eyes. "Fred, you must tell me, I need to find her, and if I can, I promise I will save the rest of those girls, your granddaughter too."

Fred shook his head, released Eleanor, and stepped away. "No Miss, the loyalists, they will take their retribution on the people of this town long after you are gone."

Eleanor considered this, perhaps the man was right, perhaps she would be putting the rest of these people in danger during her journey to save one. "Fred, if I can promise to find a way to ensure the safety of everyone, will you tell me then where the Cliffhouses are?"

He shifted on his feet; Eleanor could see the wheels turning in his mind as he considered her offer. "Cómo? How could you possibly ensure the safety of everyone?"

She patted the old man's shoulder and leaned down to whisper. "I am the aunt of Téa, the one who took down the General, I have resources. Please let me help you."

Fred relaxed and took a deep breath. "Sí, I know of Téa." He paused, deep in thought. "Miss, no 'if's'. You promise me right now to save my Amber, then I will tell you anything you want to know."

Chapter Four

Téa

Téa watched from the kitchen window of Sandstone Estate. A Gray Catbird landed on the branch of a weeping willow as the majestic tree swayed in a gentle breeze, the same Gray Catbird had shown up the day after Téa had Zephyr's memorial headstone installed. The light pink marble glimmered in the sunlight highlighting Zephyr's name.

Zephyr.

Her one and only love. Her sister, Annabelle, may have been her soulmate, but Zephyr had her heart, her desire, her hopes, and dreams. He had all of her. So, she decided to install the memorial, she would honor his memory as best she could. Then the Catbird came. She took it as a sign that he was watching over her, no matter how improbable it may be. The birds shimmering gray feathers matched Zephyr's intoxicating gray eyes. The beautiful birdsong had become a comforting familiar sound as its visits became steadier.

As she watched Ian from the kitchen window speak to the brother he would never know, her heart ached, but Téa no longer needed to look for reasons to live. She had the only thing she would ever need, Celia. Zephyr's final gift to Téa, their daughter.

Ian made his way back inside the grand castle where Téa was waiting with Emma, Ian's wife.

Emma enveloped her husband in a warm embrace. "How are you doing babe?"

Ian flashed his wife a smile and placed a kiss on her forehead. "Good, it was nice to talk to him, even if his body isn't really there. I think I needed it. It's weird to feel so much loss for someone I never even met."

Téa's heart brightened with the presence of the loving couple, even if it still stung a little to see their happiness when her chest was sore with its own missing piece.

Ian released Emma and made his way to the kitchen is-land and grabbed one of Angie's delicious homemade mixed nut banana muffins. "Where are the kids?"

Emma grabbed herself a pastry as well. She had been filling out healthily, no longer the skeletal form that she had been when Téa first met her, brushing her long yellow hair behind her shoulder, bright blue eyes shining as she spoke. "Nora is in her playpen around the corner, and Téa laid Celia down for a nap," Emma paused and rubbed her growing belly, "and this little one is kicking up a storm."

Emma laughed and pulled Ian's hand towards her bump. "See, feel right here."

They smiled together emanating joy, reveling at the life growing inside of Emma, filling the whole room with sunshine.

Téa's stomach was in knots, and her shoulders tense, tears had begun to well in her eyes, she needed to change the topic of conversation, or this sadness would consume her.

Just then little Nora cried out from the other room, saving Téa. Emma looked at Ian. "I've got her, I'm sure you two have some catching up to do anyway." Emma lifted her body from the chair and placed another kiss on her husband's cheek.

It was quiet for a moment before Ian asked. "So how are you doing, Téa?"

Téa bit back the tears that started to well up within her. "Good, we're really doing well actually. Travelling has been nice. I had always wanted to see the world, but watching life actively grow as Celia and I go to each new city... it's something I'll never tire of. Watching poppies emerge in seconds is by far my favorite. Seeing the little prickly green oval transform to a head with its brown hat, then sprouting the red petals." Téa shook her head in wonder and smiled. "I think I like it even more than seeing the trees sprout up."

She was quiet again. Ian stared at her with doubt in his eyes, so Téa continued. "But what I love even more is seeing flowing waters come back to dry land and the return of the birds." Téa stopped then before she brought up the Gray Catbird that had been visiting frequently. She didn't want

Ian to worry even more, which he might have if Téa told him that she thought the bird was a sign sent from Zephyr, or perhaps even Zephyr himself, reborn.

He had his arms and ankles crossed as he leaned back against the kitchen sink next to her. "You know sister-in-law, you don't have to be so brave all the time, it's okay to say you miss him."

"You know you don't have to call me that Ian, Zephyr and I were never married, and it's not like we were even together all that long." Téa dropped her head and wiped up imaginary crumbs from the counter with a damp rag.

Ian gently pulled her arm to force her to face him. "Téa, without a doubt, you two would have grown old together if given the chance. Time has no say when it comes to love, don't downplay what the two of you shared." He pulled her close for a hug and rubbed her arms, "Okay?"

Téa smiled and pulled away. "Okay."

"So, what are the famous Angie and William making for dinner?" Ian asked.

"I thought you and Emma had to head out early? You said you had to start nurse training with Jessop tomorrow morning."

Ian shook his head. "You're more important, I think you need us to stay awhile longer."

"Ian, no. Don't put your life on hold for me. I told you, I'm fine, I promise. I don't need a babysitter."

Ian gave her a skeptical glance and crossed his arms again.

Téa forced a chuckle. "Ian, really, Celia and I are good. She's the light of my life. Plus, Eleanor will be back soon from her trip to the east coast, and Angie and William are always here. You really don't need to worry."

Ian stood a little straighter and dropped his arms. "Okay Sis, if you say so. I guess we should pack up then, Nora's stuff fills half the backseat these days." He laughed and headed around the corner to the massive dining room where Emma and Nora played.

Téa turned back to the kitchen window and looked towards the weeping willow. The Gray Catbird appeared again, staring at her, and cooing its sweet melody. Téa took a deep breath and plastered a smile back on her face. She grasped her necklace, the rings on their silver chains, and brought them back and forth across her neck, a habit she picked up when she was no longer worried about hiding her parents' wedding bands.

It took Emma, Ian, and Téa at least an hour to load up all of Nora's baby gear that had made its way into almost every room during their stay. They had been with Téa for a week to meet their new niece, Celia. It was nice to have the company, the feeling of family as Nora's little feet padded around the Castle.

The sweeping green valley in front of Sandstone Estate was immaculate. The neatly trimmed gardens bloomed with color, and stately trees lined walking paths all around the perimeter of the estate. The gray stone castle with its sprawling towers and numerous classical windows, imposing yet welcoming. Téa had done a lot of work to turn it back into her home, the place she should have been raised if the General had not killed her parents and taken it for himself.

Ian loaded the last of their luggage into a black SUV, a gift from Téa, taken from the large fleet of vehicles left behind in Sandstone's garage. "So, Sis, will we see you again anytime soon? You haven't seen the improvements at the Sanctuary, we have an extra room for you and Celia to visit whenever you'd like."

Téa shuffled her feet, moving around small rocks that clacked together as she dug a small hole with the toe of her flat slip-on shoes. She shrugged her shoulders. "I'm not sure, maybe. We've been traveling so much; I think taking advantage of some quiet relaxation will do me some good."

Ian frowned and grabbed her shoulders. "Are you sure you don't want us to stay a while longer?"

Téa put a smile on her face and stood tall pulling him into a hug. "I'm sure, I promise, but Celia and I will be sure to come and visit as soon as that little bundle of joy decides to make their appearance."

Emma waddled over to the pair after strapping Nora into her car seat. She patted Ian on the back. "Come on babe, give Téa her space, she's strong you know." Emma winked at Téa, "She'll call us if she needs anything, won't you?" Emma narrowed her gaze and smiled at Téa.

Téa returned the grin, genuine this time. "Of course I will, promise. Now you all get going, you'll want to get through the valley before dark."

They shared one last group hug, then the Young family was on their way. Téa watched them leave until they were nothing but tail-lights in the distance. Just as she turned to make her way back inside, the baby monitor clipped to her back pocket lit up. Celia was awake from her nap.

Téa made her way to her old bedroom, where she had stayed when she first met Zephyr. Now it was Celia's nursery and Téa turned Zephyr's old room into her own. She opened the door and grabbed the plump pink bundle of rolls, Celia was a chunky baby. The infant calmed as soon as Téa picked her up, shushing her and dancing side to side. Téa sat in the rocking chair and nursed her baby girl into a calm happy stupor.

Celia had Zephyr's gray eyes, but her mother's golden skin and brown hair. Little tufts of dark curls covered her head, big clear eyes that were so alert Téa could swear she could see her child thinking. Téa cradled her daughter as she walked down to the dining room. Angie and William, the kitchen staff that had become more like family, were already seated.

Angie stood up and pulled a chair out for Téa. "Good evening you two! So happy to see little Miss tonight, I feel like she's always sleeping, I never get my cuddles." Angie reached for Celia and started cooing to the infant as she glided around the room cradling her, then looked at her husband. "William dear, will you make Téa a plate please?" Then addressing Téa. "Hun you go ahead and eat, I'll hold the little one."

Téa, immensely grateful for the help, said. "I don't know what I would do without you two, thank you."

Angie made her way back towards Téa and spoke softly in her ear. "Well, you won't ever have to find out hun. We're here to stay." She smiled and continued her slow dance around the room.

After dinner, Celia had fallen back asleep. Téa, ever so carefully, laid her back in her crib and eased the door closed. She turned the baby monitor up to the highest level to ensure she would hear Celia when she awoke and made her way down the hall to her room. Téa sat on the bed and pulled her shoes off, massaging the sore soles of her feet, and traded her clothes for silky shorts and a tank top, then curled into bed and closed her eyes.

Téa was floating in the stars, the view in front of her was of the moon and the Earth, they appeared to be the same size from this vantage point. Annabelle placed a hand on her shoulder and beamed her radiant smile.

"Beautiful up here, isn't it? It's my favorite place on the whole spaceship."

A thunderous explosion flung them sideways off their feet. Fire engulfed the air around them.

Screams echoed around the interior of the white spaceship.

The moon was splitting. Cracking in half, as flying pieces of rock slammed into the ship.

The sound of stone cracking against stone, moondust spraying in all directions.

Annabelle, blood streaming from her temple and body still as she stood facing Téa, spoke without her mouth moving. "It's coming Téa, you must be ready."

Annabelle's mouth stretching wide, a great black hole, an ear-splitting scream.

Téa woke up with a start. Heart racing, covered in sweat, Celia crying through the baby monitor. Téa hurried down the hall to her daughter's room. Only six weeks old, she had not slept through the night yet. Téa reached for her baby and nursed her through her tears. Then she walked Celia around the inner maze of Sandstone until the child was fast asleep.

Téa had just placed Celia carefully back in her crib when a quiet bell sounded from the speaker system, alerting her to someone ringing the doorbell at the front entrance. Téa's pulse quickened, and her ears filled with the sound of her own heart beating. It was the middle of the night, and no one had ever rung the front bell before, deliveries arrived in the back and her only visitors, Ian and Emma, had already gone. She regretted not keeping the General's security team, but their presence had put her on edge and Sandstone didn't feel like a home with them there.

She made her way to the front foyer and grabbed a decorative metal sword that hung over one of the many fireplaces. It was not sharp, but Téa could still bend metal to her will with her mind. She steeled herself as she came up to the front door, took a deep breath, and turned the knob.

Chapter Five
Eleanor

Bundled up in a thick warm cardigan to protect herself from the fall air, sipping her tea, Eleanor had a perfect view of the only two lodging houses in the town of St. Michaels as she watched and waited for the men who had come into Fred's place talking about the Cliffhouses. They were sure to visit again; at least that's what she was counting on. So far, it was her only lead. The old rocking chair on Fred's front porch creaked when she moved. Mist from the shipping ports surrounded the town, enveloping her like a wet blanket and softening the sounds around her. Yet, she remained alert.

When she spotted them coming, she turned her head away, pulling her sweater up to shield her face as they walked inside. Patience. Eleanor had all the patience in the world.

Eventually, the two men walked back out, their rough voices carried to Eleanor as she sat on edge waiting for them. When they were a safe distance down the street she followed them, keeping at least two blocks behind. In a town this small there weren't many other people for cover and her plan would never work if they caught her.

Eleanor thought back to three days ago when she had her conversation with Fred. He had hesitantly finished telling her what he knew about the Cliffhouses.

"What about those two men who were just here, do they work for the Cliffhouses?"

Fred shuffled his feet. "No Miss, they work for the fishing boats." Fred averted his eyes.

Eleanor bent down to meet the old man's eyes. "Please tell me, what else are you holding back?"

He sighed deeply. "They run weapons for the Loyalists."

She stood up straight, a gleam in her eye. "Which boat Fred?"

"I don't know."

Eleanor squinted her eyes at the old man, lips in a tight line. He shook his head. "I swear Miss, I avoid the pier, and if you were smart you would too."

So here she was, following the two brutes, as they scratched their asses and made bad jokes. Eleanor held back as they reached the docks. She ducked down behind an abandoned building, heart racing, and prayed no one else saw her. As soon as they boarded their ship Eleanor backed away and looked at her surroundings.

The building she was hiding behind had a window with a perfect view of the docks.

She walked around the red brick structure that had crumbled around the edges but was still standing. Eleanor pulled at the door of the building; the round knob corroded green from saltwater. Locked. She crept along the side of the building and found a window partially open. She tried to push it open carefully but it was stuck in place. Using more force this time she steadied herself, placed her elbows on the sill and her hand under the window frame, and pushed again. It gave way, opening wide enough for Eleanor to hoist herself in.

Inside, the place was littered with empty beer bottles and broken folding chairs that had collected years of dust. A burnt waste bin sat in the center of the single large empty space. Eleanor crossed to the opposite end where she could sit and watch out the low window and continue her stakeout.

The two men pulled away from the dock, and again she waited. Eleanor pulled a small bundle out of her cardigan pocket and unwrapped dried fruit that Fred had packed up for her. The old man had warmed up to her considerably over the days and even seemed hopeful about saving his granddaughter.

The sun had set, and Eleanor rubbed her arms for warmth. Her teeth chattered and legs had gone stiff. Mercifully the men finally returned. Eleanor listened as the boat engine turned off. She peeked through the window as they tied the lines. And later, she ducked down inside the building when they passed by her hiding spot.

Eleanor counted to one hundred before she unlocked the front door and left the safety of the deteriorated building.

Her flat shoes squeaked as she quickly walked down the empty promenade. A half dozen boats bumped against the dock as soft waves pushed against them. Little clouds of hot air from her lips hovered as the darkness of night enveloped her.

Eleanor took one last look around. Not a single soul was in sight. She boarded the ship and began her search; giving thanks that these men were either overconfident that no one would dare touch their territory, or just plain stupid. Either way, the lack of extra security worked in her favor. She pulled a small flashlight from her other pocket as she went below deck and methodically went inch by inch looking through the enclosed spaces. Nothing. She found nothing; despair settled around her as she resigned to reformulate her plan.

Thud, thud, thud...

Someone was above deck. Eleanor froze then quickly turned the flashlight off. She held her breath and could hear her heart pounding in her ears.

A worn-out elderly voice whispered in the dark. "Miss Eleanor, are you down there?"

Eleanor sucked in a deep breath of relief. "Fred? What on earth are you doing here?"

She heard him climb down the ladder to join her below deck. The old man's eyes were hard to make out in the dark, he gripped the sides of her arms. "I've been a bundle of nerves all day. When you didn't return to your room, I couldn't sit and wait any longer. This is the third boat I've checked. I'm so relieved to see you still standing."

Eleanor covered her eyes and sighed. "You could have gotten us both caught! It's all been pointless anyway." She dropped her hand and looked at the old man. "I haven't found anything, let's get out of here while we still can."

Fred's feet planted firmly, his rigid frame stiff from age and knees knobby, did not move out of her way as she made to leave. "Now hold on, you promised to save my granddaughter and that's exactly what you're going to do. Did you search the fish hold?"

Eleanor grunted. "You mean the stinky room with all the ice? Yeah, I checked it."

Fred gripped Eleanor's arm and pulled her forward. "Well, you didn't check it with me, I know my way around a boat, let's look again."

They reached an empty room with a single sliding aluminum door. "See?" She gestured around exasperated. "Empty. Can we please go now?"

"Wait a minute, you didn't open the door?"

Eleanor looked at him, eyes wide. "And let all the ice and fish fall out?" She placed her hands on her hips. "I do know a little about the layout of boats like this." Her cheeks warmed and she shook her head. "No, I did not open the door."

Fred limped forward and pulled the sliding door. Pounds upon pounds of ice cascaded, tinkling together as it pooled around their feet.

She gasped as the cold burned her ankles. "Fred! What did you do!? We must get out of here now!"

Fred turned to look at her. "Lower your voice and calm down, I know what I'm doing."

He started coughing, a raspy phlegmy sound, Eleanor panicked and pounded him on the back. "Fred are you okay!?"

One last deep cough. "I said lower your voice woman!" He hissed. "I'm fine, just old or couldn't you tell?"

Eleanor paused nervously and quietly chuckled. Fred started scooping away at the ice to get through the door.

"Fred, what are you doing?"

He paused, still bent over, and glanced behind him. "This room is too small; I think there's something hiding behind all this ice. Now, are you going to help me or just stand there gawking?"

Tugged out of her shock, Eleanor pulled her sleeves over her hands. "Yes, absolutely." She whispered and followed suit. Before long they uncovered a second door. They stood up breathing heavily with chilled hands and looked at one another, their apprehension sitting heavy in the air.

Eleanor pulled the second sliding door, and inside was a room full of shelves and wooden crates. It was stuffed full of artillery. Ammunition, firearms, even grenades. Everything Eleanor could possibly need to take over the loyalists, if only she had some help, perhaps she'd have to reach out to her niece for some backup.

Fred smiled wide, his wrinkles forming cat whiskers across his face. "Now, let's see if we can't find something to load this onto."

Eleanor started laughing again and held her hand to her mouth, overcome with joy she hugged the old man.

He cringed under her embrace. "Easy now woman! You're crushing my bones."

It took the pair most of the night to get everything they could back to Fred's place. He had an old van that he rarely used due to the lack of fuel availability. But it had enough gas to make the trip to the docks and back.

Eleanors' pulse raced the entire time. Sure they would be caught any second, but luck was on their side that night.

When they got back to Fred's place, they pulled the loaded van into his garage. When the old man opened the side door to his house, Eleanor's mouth dropped open. There were no fewer than twenty people packed into the old man's tiny kitchen.

Eleanor looked around in surprise. "Fred, what is this?"

He held his arms open wide and gestured to the crowd. "This... is every parent, friend, lover, and ally we have in this fight." Fred turned to look at Eleanor, a sadness around his eyes. "It's what we should have done months ago, come together to get our girls back." His shoulders dropped as he continued. "When you didn't return earlier today, I went to every person in this town that I knew I could trust." He raised his head high. "I've waited far too long to do something about those wretched men who took our children, you inspired me, Eleanor. You are not alone."

Eleanor's skin tingled and her eyes glimmered, she looked to the crowd. "Thank you. Thank you for helping me."

Fred led her over to a couple near the back of the room. "Eleanor, I'd like you to meet Richard and Kimberly."

Eleanor smiled and stuck out her hand. "It's nice to meet you both."

The couple shook her hand but did not smile in return. "The loyalists, they took our boy, we're here to help get him back."

Her heart dropped to her knees. "I don't understand, I thought the loyalist just took the girls...to force them to reproduce."

Richard and Kimberly looked at each other. Kimberly shook her head. "No, not just the girls. They took our boys too. They're still testing Connex-B genes."

Eleanor's stomach clenched and she felt the blood leave her face. "I'm... I'm so sorry." She hated herself for a moment; for ever serving the General. Even if she didn't have a hand in the Connex experiments, she chided herself for every email he had dictated to her, every cup of coffee she ever brought him, every employee she ever hired to help assist the upkeep of Sandstone estate. Even if she didn't have a child of her own, she too should have fought back sooner.

Kimberly started to cry, and Richard rubbed her back. Eleanor patted her on the shoulder. "Don't worry, we'll get them back, we'll get all of them back."

CHAPTER SIX
Theo

Theo pulled the rusted old truck into a parking space in front of the hardware store. The engine grumbled to a stop and the truck door whined as Theo got out. He walked around the truck to the passenger side and helped Elijah down, then passed him his crutches.

Inside, Theo asked to use the telephone. He called Elijah's parents, grateful that they were part of the rehabilitation program and had a working landline, as well as most of the businesses around town.

Theo glanced at Elijah as he hung up, placing the old phone on its receiver, its long cord twirling down the wall. He walked over and crouched down to look at the young boy. "Well kid, pretty sure you're grounded for a month, so let's make the best of it." He clapped Elijah on the back.

"How about we come back for your Dad's order, and we see if the library has any new issues of, 'Dr. Symbico vs. Sir Featisvus'?"

Elijah's face lit up. "Thanks Theo, you're the best!"

Theo laughed, a warm and hearty sound. "You know what else? I don't think I've ever had ice cream." Theo winked and tousled Elijah's hair as they made their way back out to the street.

The Town center was small. Shops lined the main street, but most were still empty. Most of the people walked or biked, not many were using vehicles again yet, even though the world was getting back to what it used to be before The Decline.

Theo and Elijah crossed main street to get to the library a few blocks down. A great sense of peace washed over Theo as he took in the smell of the rows and rows of books lining the shelves. He grinned and led Elijah to the racks of magazines and comic books.

They passed a grand spiral staircase that climbed to the upper level that was closed to the public. Suddenly fear tensed Theo's shoulders as if on instinct. Something about the spiral staircase and all the books put him on edge, looking for signs of danger. He shook off a chill and smiled at Elijah who was practically bouncing with excitement.

After the library, they went down the street to get two scoops of ice cream. Theo tried not to cringe as he handed over the precious dollars he had been saving for his shirt and hat. It was worth it to see the joy radiating out of Elijah.

Melted mint chocolate chip ran down Elijah's small hand as the two sat outside soaking up the sun. "This is the best day ever! Thanks Theo!"

"You're welcome kid, just don't do it again okay?" He chuckled. "Or your Ma will probably throw me out."

When they finished eating, they made their way back to the hardware store, which was also a general store, and picked up what Phil had ordered. The owner assisted while Theo loaded the water heater into the back of the old pick-up truck and helped to strap it down.

On the way back to the farm Elijah giggled and flew his hand like an airplane out of the window trying to catch the wind, while Theo sang to the music.

They were halfway home when Elijah stilled. His eyes went wide. Theo turned the music down. "Elijah? What's wrong kid?"

Elijah didn't respond. He gripped his seat tight, and his body shook.

"ELIJAH!" Theo screamed.

Theo slammed on the brakes, jumped out of the truck, and ran to the passenger door. As he swung it open, Elijah finally moved and looked at Theo. "Didn't you hear her Theo?"

"Hear who kid?" His voice was almost a scream. "What just happened?"

Elijah turned his seated body towards Theo as his shaking stopped. "The lady, in the radio. She said that you need to go home now. That Téa is waiting for us."

Theo shook his head and stared desperately at the young boy. "Téa? Who's Téa? What lady?"

Elijah smiled and relaxed his body. "It's okay Theo, she's nice. She said Téa would know what to do. We have to go to Sandstone Estate."

"Kid, you're not making any sense. Maybe you hit your head too hard earlier in the back of the truck. Let's get you home, your mom and dad can call your doctor."

Theo turned Elijah back in his seat making sure his legs were clear of the truck door and shut it tight. He was walking around the front of the truck when a loud reverberating crack, so loud it was like the Earth was split in half, stopped him in his tracks. His heart rate ramped up, then a thundering boom shook the ground beneath him. He tried to steady himself on the shaky pavement and looked ahead. A shockwave of fire screamed down the road towards them. Theo ran and jumped into the truck. Heart pounding out of his chest, he pulled Elijah down beneath the long bench seat and the boy screamed. The truck rattled as the force of an explosion hurtled past them. Wind filled with dirt flew at the truck rocking it side to side, debris flowed in through the open window.

Finally, just when he thought he could take no more, the air calmed. Theo lifted his head, and sand fell from his hair. He helped Elijah back into his seat. Theo's jaw dropped as he looked out of the windshield. In front of them as far as the eye could see there was a sea of red and brown clouds, like a dirty fog. Theo closed his mouth and gulped down the fear for the sake of the small boy seated next to him. The land was flattened, no grass, no trees stood; all of it lay burnt against the ground. He drummed the steering wheel thinking they needed to get help but the roadway behind them now had great impassable crevasses torn into the Earth.

Theo scooted back behind the wheel and turned the key in the ignition. Gratefully the engine roared to life, and he sighed deeply with relief. He drove slowly and carefully, avoiding downed power lines and fallen trees until they reached the road that would lead them to the farmhouse. Theo was forced to stop the truck miles away from the farmhouse. Heat blasted them with the force of an inferno. The house was about three miles out, but he could see from where they were forced to stop, that there was nothing left. A great pit was where the house used to be, a giant rock in its place. The farm, and everything surrounding it, had been hit by a meteor.

Theo looked at Elijah as tears streamed down his young dirt-covered face.

"What do we do now Theo?" Elijah hiccupped.

Theo's thoughts were muddled, he knew he should be comforting the boy who was so suddenly an orphan. Perhaps trying again to find another way back to town to seek out help, but he couldn't bring himself to think clearly. He could only hear Elijah's voice in his head saying, *Téa would know what to do.* "I guess we're going to Sandstone Estate."

Chapter Seven
Eleanor

Once the townspeople opened up to her, information flowed freely. The Cliffhouses it turned out, were not houses at all, but a network of tunnels carved into the side of a cliff overlooking the ocean, what used to be Clavert Cliffs State park. It didn't take long to formulate a plan and put it into action.

The night was clear. The moon and stars illuminated the ocean water as Eleanor and the townspeople dropped anchor near the bottom of a massive cliff. A forest of trees topped the looming rock face that stretched above them.

The night was still, and the water calm. An eerie silence enveloped Eleanor and a half dozen of the parents of St. Michaels. They were crouched inside a large fishing boat that belonged to Richard and Kimberly, the parents of one of the stolen boys.

There was a staircase that was carved into the side of the rock that began at the bottom of the cliff by the ocean's edge and rose to the top. The tunnels could only be accessed from an entrance at the top of the cliffs hidden in the trees. Richard had previously gathered intel for his own failed rescue. He had made it all the way to the top of the Cliffhouses unseen, but when he saw the numerous armed men, he turned back. His information was invaluable to them now.

They all gathered into a smaller boat to get closer to the shore. Richard beached them next to the staircase. Eleanor and the parents checked the ammunition of each of their stolen guns. One by one they started their climb to the top. Eleanor steadied her stance with each step as she walked the slimy surface. The footholds were small and lumpy from being poorly hand-carved and covered with algae. She had to swing her rifle to her back and use her hands as well as her feet to climb the stairs.

Her heart raced and a whooshing in her ears began to drown out all other noise. This seemed too easy. Where were the guards? How had she and Fred stolen the weapons so easily? When she finally reached the top, out of breath and sweat pouring down the sides of her face, she peeked over the edge. The trees were dense, and she couldn't see much further than a few feet.

Silence.

Where were all the armed guards? She carefully pulled herself over the top and crawled on the forest floor before coming to a stance. Moss and pine needles carpeted the forest floor. She took cover behind the closest tree and looked at her surroundings. There was not a single person in sight. She whistled a short two-tone melody to signal to the others that the coast was clear.

As the last person climbed to the top of the stairs a blinding white floodlight illuminated the forest. A booming voice echoed through speakers all around them.

"DROP YOUR WEAPONS OR WE WILL SHOOT!"

Eleanor stood frozen, gripping her weapon stunned. Eyes wide, her hands began to shake, heart beating fast.

"DROP YOUR WEAPONS NOW, FINAL WARNING!"

Clink-clink-clink-thud-thud-thud.

Dirt sprayed her eyes and the person on her right dropped to the ground. Two more fell back behind her over the top of the cliff plunging down to the depths of the cold ocean below. More bodies fell as round after round hit their intended targets.

Eleanor's jaw locked and her whole body trembled, still she clung frozen to her rifle.

When the shooting stopped, a broad tall man stomped slowly towards her. He was nothing but a shadow silhouette with the blinding light flooding the night from behind him. "This one goes to the Cliffhouses. Tie her hands."

Someone easily tugged the rifle from her frozen grasp and lifted it from the strap around her body. Then another man tied her hands behind her back. He shoved her roughly forward. "*Move!*" he growled.

Eleanor fell to her knees and one of the men kicked her in the ribs. She gasped, clutching the burning sting in her torso, a silent scream escaped her. Her captor shoved her face into the dirt then yanked her head back up by the hair. He spat in her face. "I *said move.*"

Eleanor struggled to her feet, each step like moving through sludge as the man kept a tight grip on her forearm. She chanced a glance behind her and saw Fred, also tied up and bleeding from the head. They were the only two left.

Bile filled her throat, and she swallowed it back, stomach-churning, they were going to die tonight. Téa, Celia, Mabel, she would never see their beautiful faces again. Despair settled in her chest; her lungs started to burn.

They finally reached the entrance to the caves, and everything went dark.

The Loyalists all pulled night vision goggles over their eyes as they entered the tunnels. Each time Eleanor tripped, the guard pulled her roughly back to her feet and slapped her across the face. Quiet tears streamed down her cheeks.

After several minutes she was shoved into an alcove. The cold feel of metal against her skin made her heart leap, but it was only the guard cutting her wrists free. She could not see a thing, but could hear the squeal of metal hinges slamming shut and heavy footsteps walking away. She was alone.

She felt around, taking small steps, scared of falling suddenly into an unseen hole. But the ground was solid. She moved until she felt the cool rough surface of a curved rock wall and slid down it. She wrapped her arms around her legs and allowed the sadness to overtake her.

What was she thinking? She never should have believed she could succeed in this rescue mission. It was her fault all those people died; all their children were orphans now.

She sobbed, but her wails were silenced when she heard an old voice not far away.

"Eleanor?" The old voice asked.

She couldn't believe her ears. "Fred?" A smile spread across her face knowing the old man was alive and close by, in a different cell.

"Yes, it's me. Don't waste your tears on those, pinche pendejos, evil sacks of meat, they aren't worth it, Nelly."

"Nelly?"

"Yeah, you seem like a nervous Nelly, it's fitting for you."

Eleanor laughed, some of the tension leaving her body. "What happened to Miss?"

"I think we're past polite titles don't you think?"

Eleanor chuckled again. "I suppose you're right. Where are you?"

The old man's voice sounded heavy. "Across the hall I think, I can't see my own hand in front of my face."

The moment of relief seeped away, and despair crept back in. "Me either. I'm so sorry Fred, I should have listened to you. I never should have gotten involved, all those people, those parents..."

"Now Nelly, don't you dare put this on yourself. It is no one's fault except for the loyalists. They are the only ones to blame here, do you hear me?"

Eleanor could hear the anger and frustration seeping from the old man. "I hear you, Fred." She sighed deeply. "What do we do now?"

He was quiet before answering. "Well, I know what we don't do, and that's give up, do you hear me, Nelly? You just hold tight, and something will turn in our favor, it must. You just hold onto your hope."

"Poppa?"

Eleanor's heart jumped to her throat. Excitement raced through her veins.

Fred's old voice thick with surprise. "Amber? Is that really you mija?"

A beautiful strong voice echoed from somewhere further down from Fred. "Yes, Poppa it's me!"

"Gracias a Dios! My girl, my beautiful girl." Eleanor could hear Fred's words through his elated sobs. "Are you okay? Are you hurt?"

Amber's voice carried. "I'm okay Poppa, I'm okay." Her words hitched in her throat. "I'm not hurt... physically, I don't think so anyway."

Suddenly a different rough loud voice boomed in the dark. "No *talking*!"

Fred's voice turned to pure anger. "You let us out, or I swear to God I'll kill every last one of you."

There was a shuffling sound of feet on dirt, then the metal squeal of hinges opening. The rough voice boomed again. *"Did you really just threaten me, old man!"*

Eleanor could hear the two men grappling, then she could hear the wet sound of a knife penetrating flesh. Amber screamed in the darkness and Eleanor shouted. "STOP IT! LET HIM GO!"

She jumped to her feet and sprinted to her cage doors, shaking them as hard as she could, but it was useless, the doors would not budge.

The gurgling from Fred stopped, and the sound of a body dropping to the floor was sickening.

Another scream from Amber, but this one echoed around them like a thousand screams from all directions. The floor shook and the shrieking dug into Eleanor's ears like painful pinpricks stabbing in, and she clapped her hands to the sides of her head to block the noise.

Then a beautiful glow flowed from down the tunnel, it was a brilliant pink light spreading to every crevice. Eleanor looked through her cell bars and saw a gorgeous young woman floating down the hall, arms outstretched to her sides, feet dangling inches from the floor.

The armed guard raised his gun and started to shoot at her repeatedly, but the bullets dropped like flies that flattened on impact against an invisible shield.

The girl landed in front of the armed guard. She swung an arm out in front of her towards the guard so quickly Eleanor almost didn't register it. Her fingers stretched outwards like long fleshy vines and wrapped themselves around the guard's throat. His gun clattered to the ground, and he gasped for air. She raised her other arm and it too snaked out and wrapped itself around the guard's body multiple times, squeezing its prey until his bloodied eyes popped out millimeters from where they should be.

The young woman, who must be Amber, softly landed. Her fingers and arm shrunk back to their normal lengths and the guard fell dead to the floor. Eleanor stood watching through the bars with her mouth agape. Amber turned to face Eleanor, snapped her fingers and the metal bars vanished. Then Amber's eyes closed, and she collapsed against Eleanor.

Chapter Eight
Theo

As Theo started to drive away from the devastation the meteor had left in its wake, he trembled. *How are we going to make it all the way to Sandstone Estate?*

He had very little money saved up, especially after splurging on the ice cream cones earlier today. He *maybe* had enough for one tank of gas. Let alone the cost of food, water, and a place to sleep. Sandstone Estate was well known, Téa was a sort of interim president, so finding it would not be a problem. The problem was getting there, the journey would take at least two days, even with the adrenaline currently coursing through his veins, there was no way he could drive straight there without stopping to rest.

Maybe the kid has extended family who could take us in?

Theo looked to him. "Hey Elijah buddy, are you okay kiddo?"

Elijah sniffled in response and looked out his window.

Theo gripped the steering wheel tighter, then relaxed his shoulders. "I'm so sorry little man... do you know of any other family out there? Aunts, uncles, cousins?"

Elijah shook his head in response as he continued to stare out the truck window.

Theo cleared his throat and smiled. "Well, we have each other, right?" When Elijah still didn't say anything, Theo continued. "I was wondering, do you remember the last scene we read from Dr. Symbico vs. Sir Festivus?" Still no response. "I just can't seem to remember, who made it first to the transfiguration potion that would open up the doorway to the hidden world?"

Still, nothing but silence.

God, I suck at this. Leave the poor kid alone, he just lost his whole world. Shit. I just lost my whole world.

Keeping one eye on the road, Theo ejected the cassette tape he and Elijah had been listening to and scanned the radio stations. He turned the dial over and over, praying for some kind of emergency broadcast that would tell him what to do. Hoping that maybe there was some other person out there who knew how to adult better than him. His hope sank when he heard nothing but static.

What am I going to do?

After hours of driving, the dry farm fields that expanded as far as the eye could see, slowly began to be replaced with the occasional house or deserted convenience store. They were coming up to the town neighboring the one they left behind. Many cities were deserted during The Decline as the population decreased. This city ahead had once been a major metropolis, with towering skyscrapers. But now it had nature growing up the sides of those skyscrapers, creating monstrous shadows that crept over them. Half-crumbled structures that had fallen apart from neglect, littered out into the streets. Most major cities became too difficult to upkeep as the population decreased, and the capitals of today were mostly much smaller well-maintained towns. However, there were rumors of people who squatted in the ghost cities, waiting to attack unsuspecting passersby. Like trolls under a bridge, taking their tolls and surviving on their spoils.

Theo was already on high alert from the meteor impact, but that feeling amplified as they entered the desecrated business sector. If only there was a way around, but this was the only paved way through. His heart raced, and his eyes swept their surroundings as he drove. There were so many blind corners where evil could be lurking. His right foot on the gas and his left foot tapping an invisible drum on the floorboards. The sooner they passed through this asphalt jungle and onto the next viable hub, the better.

Theo tried to talk to Elijah again as a distraction from the anxiety he was feeling, the kid must be scared too, maybe talking would calm them both. "So, I hear Sandstone Estate is so big, that you could fit thirty normal sized houses inside of it! Can you believe that? I bet–"

POP!

The truck swerved to one side, tires squealing, threatening to tip over. Elijah screamed. Theo held fast to the wheel, keeping them upright as the tail end swayed back and forth, Theo shot his right arm out across Elijah's chest. They came to an abrupt halt.

"Elijah! Are you okay?"

Elijah shook in his seat, new tears spilled down his cheeks, a deafening cry, but no words, came from his mouth.

Cha. Click. The sound of a gun being loaded froze Theo to his seat.

A stranger's thick voice growled at them. "Hands up! Don't move!"

Theo's voice quavered. "Please, we don't have–"

"QUIET, I didn't say you could talk!" The stranger yelled. "Now, get out slowly or I'll shoot you and the boy."

Before Theo could even process the full sentence being spoken to him, as if on instinct, he flung open his door, hitting the man in the gut. Heart racing and mind sharp, Theo's body knew what to do. The stranger bent over and stumbled backward, then with muscles taut, Theo kicked him hard in the chest. The man gasped and grunted then dropped his rifle. Theo swiftly retrieved it and pressed the barrel to his assailant's temple.

Theo's words came out controlled and like ice, a vein in his neck throbbed. "*My turn.* Get up."

The stranger slowly wobbled to his feet and Theo prodded him in the back with his weapon.

"Who else is with you?" Theo demanded.

The man spat in reply, and Theo slammed the butt end of the gun against the man's head. One drop of blood trickled down from his hairline. The stranger staggered and Theo asked again. "*Who else?*"

Through gritted teeth, the man claimed. "No one, I live out here alone."

"We'll see about that." Theo looked back at the truck. "Elijah, you stay put, I'll be right back."

Elijah was sobbing, eyes wide with fear, he gripped the edge of the open truck window, finally, Elijah spoke. "P-p-please don't leave me, Theo."

Guilt waved at Theo like a demon waiting in the shadows. *I'm sorry you have to see me like this Elijah.*

Theo's words were a low growl in the man's ear. "Take me to your house, *now*, or I'll put a bullet in each kneecap and leave you here to rot." Theo jabbed at the man's back again.

The stranger, stubborn like a mule, did not budge. "Look man, I get how this looks, but I'm not what you think I am. If you really want me to take you to where I'm holed up, you'll want to bring the kid, it won't be safe to leave him here."

Theo ground his teeth, debating. *What if it's a trap and Elijah gets hurt? What if I leave him and something does happen to Elijah because I'm not here? Maybe I should take the gun and just keep driving, damnit we can't drive the truck now, we won't make it without supplies.*

"Okay, but one wrong move from you, and I will not hesitate to take you down."

The man nodded his head. "I understand."

The trio slowly walked past building after building, the shadows grew longer and darker. An orange glow from the setting sun cast eerie rainbows through the tall broken glass of fractured municipal towers.

Theo glanced at Elijah. He could see the strain in the boys' eyes, all this walking was taking its toll. "How much further?" Theo asked.

"Not much, two more blocks." The stranger answered.

The last rays of the day finally faded, and Theo could hardly see where he was going every time a building blocked out the light from the moon. He was starting to worry about Elijah's stability on his crutches. "How you doing over there little man?"

Elijah was a couple of feet to the side. Theo still had his aim set on the stranger as they walked. Elijah shrugged in response to the question.

"We have arrived gentlemen!" The man clapped his hands together and rubbed them back and forth in a frenzy. "What a treat to have guests, it's been so long."

Every alarm bell started to ring in Theo's mind. *This guy is crazy.* "Where exactly is 'here'?"

Shoulder-length black hair and a grizzly-like beard obscured most of the stranger's face, but Theo could see the whites of his teeth formed in the shape of a smile, with bright green cat-like eyes that shone in the darkness. He held his arms out wide. "Welcome. To the 'Museum of Nature and Science', watch your step."

They had walked through an airy opening where glass doors once stood. Inside, a T-Rex skeleton, at least fifteen feet high, hovered over them. Its yellowed pointed teeth and sharp claws loomed above their heads, poised and ready to take down its prey. Moss covered the floors and an earthen scent filled Theo's nose.

Theo's grip wavered on the rifle. "Really? You live here?"

The bear-like man grinned in response. "You betcha! Since The Decline. Someone must keep history alive!" He paused and scratched at a scab on top of one hand. "Of course, there used to be more of us, Generals men came-"

The mans speech came out fast and started stringing together, he rambled, and Theo was losing his patience, Elijah needed to rest. "That's enough! Where do you keep the supplies you've stolen!?"

The man looked at Theo, incredulous. "Stolen? I've never stolen from travelers, I'm not a scavenger!"

Theo renewed his grip on the gun. "Then why did you take out our tires!? Why threaten us!?"

The stranger was shaking. "I know, I know how it looks. But you see, I felt the vibrations, that aftershock was no earthquake. I would know. Dunamis must have set off another nuke. I needed information... and you looked...familiar. I thought you were one of them."

If this guy really was a scavenger, I would not have been able to overtake him so easily, plus he's acting like he hasn't seen another human in years. Theo lowered the weapon but did not give it back. Thick sarcasm laced Theo's voice as he said. "Well good news is you're wrong about that shock you felt. It was no bomb. It was a meteorite."

The man took a step back, eyes wide, and gripped the sides of his head. "Holy hell."

Theo wanted to tell the man more, explain how it took out their home and Elijah's parents. But he was already worried about Elijah, and he didn't need to bring that up, not now. "Look man, we really need a place to rest, and considering you took out our transportation, you owe us. Do you have something to eat? A place to sleep?"

The man stood unresponsive in his shock, and Theo's frustration grew. "Dude! Over here, look at me man. What's your name?"

The stranger looked at Theo and dropped his hands back down to his sides. "Rigel, my name is Rigel."

Theo took a deep breath. "That's great, nice to meet you Rigel. My name is Theo, and this is Elijah. Can you help us out here?"

He nodded his head. "Yes, yes, right this way."

As the man started to walk away, Theo heard an echoing clatter behind him, he turned just in time to see Elijah had dropped one of his crutches and was beginning to fall over. Theo rushed to his side and caught the boy. "Elijah!"

Elijah's eyes rolled to the back of his head, a faint sheen of sweat on his brow glistened in the moonlight. Theo shouted. "Elijah!"

The boy groaned and opened his eyes halfway. "Theo. Theo, I'm tired, and my head hurts."

Theo's heart began to race. "It's alright little man, I've got you, it's going to be okay."

Rigel rushed to their side, and Theo tensed, he had dropped the gun.

But Rigel picked the rifle up and put the strap over Theo's head and shoulder and said. "Come on, this way, there's a bunk room for the employees who used to work the night shifts."

Theo let out a breath of relief and followed him down the long wide corridors of the neglected museum. Spacious skylights overhead let the moonshine through and cast long shadows as they passed by the various exhibits. Nature had taken back the food court. Greenery grew between the cracks in the tile, and up the base of chairs and tables, turning the room into one big modern forest.

They passed by environmentally sealed display cases, their interiors perfectly preserved and filled with long extinct animals, a woolly mammoth, saber tooth cat, and dodo birds. All of which were surrounded by the environments they would have lived in.

When they finally reached a steel door with a simple plaque that said, 'EMPLOYEES ONLY', Rigel went through first and held it open for Theo. As the door slowly squeaked shut, darkness enveloped them. Theo could hear his heart pounding in his ears, and then Rigel turned on a flashlight.

"Come on, this way, not much further." Rigel said.

The plain hallway had doors lining each side, after only a handful of feet Rigel stopped in front of one and pushed it open. Once Theo was inside with Elijah, Rigel went towards a counter and turned on a lantern which illuminated the entire room with a soft light. There were four sets of bunk beds, a small kitchen, and even a restroom off to the side, its door slightly ajar.

Rigel addressed Theo. "So, what's up with him?"

Theo was still looking around the room. "I'm sorry what?"

"The kid, what's wrong with him?"

Theo looked at the man with steel in his eyes. "Nothing, nothing is wrong with him." He spat.

The man raised his hands in surrender. "I didn't mean anything by it, I just meant maybe I could help if I knew his condition." He grinned widely and pointed a finger at his own chest. "I used to be a scientist you know." He wiggled his eyebrows.

Theo leaned away from Rigel and sighed. "He has early onset multiple sclerosis."

Rigel whistled a long sharp tune. "Oh man, I'm sorry."

Theo dropped his shoulders but kept his grip tight on Elijah. "Thanks. His parents joined the rehabilitation program, you know, farming. Trying to bring the Earth back to life." Theo brought Elijah, who had fallen asleep, to one of the beds and laid him down. Rigel sat on a neighboring bed, and Theo continued to talk. "The program paid for his medical care. Of course, there's no cure, but the treatments had been helping his nerve inflammation. We've been through so much in just one day, plus the long walk. It took a lot out of him. You don't have any first aid, do you? Some pain killers maybe?"

Rigel jumped to his feet. "Yeah, yeah, actually I do."

He rummaged through a cabinet and brought back a small jar of aspirin and a bottle of water.

Theo gently shook Elijah's shoulder to wake him, and he sat up groggily. "Hey buddy, take this, it'll help you sleep better, you won't wake up in as much pain, okay little man?"

Elijah nodded and swallowed the pill, then laid back down.

With Elijah asleep, Theo looked to Rigel. "So, you want to tell me about yourself? Like why you're living in a museum alone?"

Rigel sat back down, and rubbed his knees, he stared towards the ceiling and sighed. "God, it's been so long, sometimes I don't even know anymore why I'm here." He took a deep breath and continued. "There used to be dozens of us, scientists, researchers. The museum was safer to work in than our labs, no one looked here when it was shut down. When The Decline was happening, we kept working, looking for a cure, a reason for what was happening. We knew humans were destroying the planet, but no one had guessed the main catalyst was an invisible poison seeping through our pores.

"By the time we figured it out, the damage was done. We couldn't change human nature. So, a few of us left to live out our lives as best we could, but some of us stayed. We decided to attempt to preserve the history within these walls.

"Then Dunamis came. Something big had happened and they needed new scientists. Someone had ratted us out."

Rigel whimpered. "They took them. I was out on a supply run, and when I came back, I saw the soldiers loading my friends into the back of big black SUV's." Rigel kept talking through sobs. "I should have followed them; I should have saved them. But I'm not a fighter, they would have just taken me too." He raised his head and looked Theo in the eyes. "I was alone after that, for a long time. Then I felt the shockwave. And I knew I had to do something. I had to fight back. That's when you two came along."

Theo was quiet for a minute before responding, wondering how much he should share. But he needed this man to trust him. Elijah needed his help. "I woke up in a hospital, with no memory of my life. I was assigned to work a farm with Elijah here and his family, we were on our way home when the meteor hit." Theo reached for Rigel's shoulder and patted him on the back. "Dunamis is gone, well, the General is gone. From what I've been told, the people who took over are good. They started the rehabilitation program to start growing the earth again. There's no one left to fight, Rigel."

The man stood and shook his head. "No, no, how could you know that? Why take my friends then? It was only months ago, or was it years? Maybe it was yesterday? How could you know, some farmer with no memory!? You couldn't know what they're capable of."

Rigel paced, eyes wild, and spittle sticking to his beard. Theo stood and calmly raised his hands. "You're right, you're right, I couldn't possibly know. Why don't you take it easy, Rigel?"

The man paused and looked at Theo. "Sorry, sorry. Hey, so what about you and the kid? What are you doing all the way out here?"

Theo dared not to trust this man with where they were headed and why, he already seemed a little on edge without hearing about messages coming from a radio that only Elijah could hear. "Well, the meteorite I told you about, it hit the farm where we lived. We were lucky not to have been home at the time. We're traveling to some relatives on the east coast."

Rigel sat back down and nodded his head, swaying slowly backwards and forwards. "Right, right, yeah, that makes sense. Skip town before the chaos comes."

Theo narrowed his eyes at Rigel's fidgeting form, and carefully asked. "So hey," he hesitated, "you don't have any supplies that you could part with, do you?"

Rigel stopped swaying and snapped his head up. "You after my research!?"

Theo put his hands out placating. "No, not at all, I just meant, are there any abandoned vehicles around here that might have usable tires, gas, food, anything that might help us get on our way?"

We are not staying here tonight. I'll let Elijah rest a few hours while I gather supplies.

Rigel relaxed. "Oh, yes, right, of course, supplies." He looked around the room in thought. "Yes, actually, before the soldiers came, the others and I had accumulated quite the stash if you know what I mean." Rigel winked.

Theo smiled. "That's great Rigel, do you think you could show me?"

Rigel jumped up. "Yes, yes, right this way."

"Okay, hold on just a minute. Let me tell Elijah, I don't want him to wake up scared and alone."

Theo gently gave Elijah a pat on the arm, rousing him from his sleep. "Hey kiddo, Rigel has some supplies for us, I'm going to go with him, but I want you to stay here and rest."

Elijah's eyes widened in panic. "No, I want to go with you."

Theo gently held Elijah's arm. "I need you to stay here and rest little man, but I promise, I'll be back soon."

A single tear ran down Elijah's cheek. "You promise you won't leave without me?"

Theo smiled. "I promise, I will never leave you, it's you and me, always. I'll be right back."

Elijah nodded his head and sniffled before laying back down. Theo gestured to Rigel, "Okay, let's go."

The two men continued to walk down the dark employee hallway lit by the flashlight Rigel carried. When they reached the end Rigel pushed open the last door. In front of them was an expansive loading dock piled high with boxes and some heavy equipment.

Rigel grinned mischievously at Theo. "See, we've got everything you need here."

Theo's pulse quickened and he clapped Rigel on the back. "This is great! Can you lead me to a working vehicle and help me load it up?"

Rigel squinted his eyes at Theo and stiffened his posture. "Are you after my research!?"

Theo stood his ground, and spoke softly. "No Rigel, remember, you are helping me and Elijah. A working car with gas, some food, and clean water?"

Rigel nodded his head. "Right, right, yes, this way."

Theo clenched and unclenched his hands, gritting his teeth as he followed Rigel towards the front of the loading docks, towards the exit.

We've got to get out of here.

Rigel opened a side door and propped it open with a brick. "Here you are my friend, take your pick!"

A cool night breeze swept over his skin, Theo sucked in the fresh air and sighed in relief. In front of him, parked outside, were three vehicles that looked well maintained. A mid-size car, a truck, and a van. Just then Theo heard the brick scrape against the concrete behind him.

Rigel Screamed. "I WON'T LET YOU STEAL MY RE-SEARCH!" And the door slammed shut.

Fuck.

Theo raced along the outside of the building, looking for another way to get in. His shoes slapped the pavement, and his breath came in hard and ragged.

Elijah, I have to get to Elijah.

Finally, he found a window that was low enough to jump through, where the glass was already blown out. He sailed through, landing on the other side with a tuck and roll. He leapt up and continued his sprint back, scanning the walls for any door that would lead to the employee corridors. He ran at full speed in the darkness, pushing as fast as he could towards the center of the museum, when suddenly he tripped over a fallen mummy sarcophagus.

His knees hit the floor hard, and the momentum pitched him forward, he landed hard on his shoulder with a sickening pop. His shoulder was dislocated. He groaned, got up, and kept running. He rounded a corner and at last, came to a door with an 'EMPLOYEES ONLY' plaque.

Theo backed up and looked at the sharp edge of the wall to the side of the door. He took three deep breaths...

1...

2...

3...

Then slammed his shoulder against the edge, popping his shoulder back into place. He shouted profanities he didn't even realize he had. He then turned back around and flung the door open. He continued his sprint into the pitch-black corridor.

Light from the lantern in the bunk room flooded from under the door. Theo slowly turned the handle and carefully opened the door. Elijah sat crying on the bed, Rigel had his arms tightly wrapped around the boy, squeezing him too hard.

Theo raised his hands slowly out in front of him. "Easy Rigel, take it easy. Just let him go and we'll leave."

Rigel shouted at Theo. "Who are you!? What do you want!?"

Theo eyed the Rifle on the floor across from Rigel and took one step towards it. "Nothing, we don't want anything from you, we were just leaving."

Rigel screamed. "You're not taking my research!"

In swift movements Theo grabbed the barrel of the gun and swung the grip end at the man's head, striking him unconscious. He slumped backwards on the bed releasing Elijah and a small pool of blood formed under Rigel's head.

Okay, more than unconscious.

Elijah sobbed and reached for Theo. He picked the boy up and moved him to another bed, then quickly searched the cabinets above and below the long countertop. He thanked whatever God might be listening when he found a box with bottles of water, a can opener, and canned food. Theo grabbed the aspirin and placed it in the box, then went back to Elijah.

"Do you think you could walk again, little man?"

Elijah nodded his head and wiped his nose with his sleeve. Theo handed him his crutches and they made their way out of the room and back to the selection of cars.

As they drove away from the museum in a minivan, adrenaline leaving his body, Theo trembled behind the steering wheel. He didn't know what to say to Elijah. He turned the radio on and tried scanning the channels.

Elijah perked up from where he was laying down in the backseat. "Theo?"

Theo cleared his throat and looked in the rearview mirror. "Yeah, little man?"

"Annabelle says not to worry. She says Téa's not like that man, she says Sandstone is our home now. It'll be okay there Theo."

He could only nod his head in reply, the lump in his throat blocking his words. He reached behind his seat and ruffled Elijah's hair.

After Elijah had fallen asleep, Theo pulled to the side of the road and allowed himself to cry. After several minutes, he shook off the stress consuming him.

I must be strong for Elijah.

With renewed determination, Theo continued driving. He promised himself to take a leap of faith and put all his trust in Elijah, he would believe that Sandstone could be their new home.

Despite his exhaustion, Theo refused to stop again, except to relieve themselves. The cans of food were inedible, they had long expired and smelled ripe when Theo opened them. It was the next night by the time they finally reached the giant castle. Their stomachs clenched in hunger, a thin layer of dirt and grime covered their clothing, and Theo was having a hard time keeping his eyes open.

Theo and Elijah got out of the van and walked towards the massive front door.

Please let this work out okay, please let the owner be a good, sane person. Please, we need a break.

Theo took a deep breath and rang the doorbell.

CHAPTER NINE
Téa

When Téa opened the front door, the decorative metal sword dropped from her hands and clattered to the ground. Her fingers trembled as she raised them to her face and covered her mouth.

She must still be dreaming... Annabelle was screaming in her dream telling her 'it was coming', was this the 'it'? Was Zephyr really back from the dead? Or maybe it wasn't Zephyr at all, but a three-headed monster about to transform and gobble her up right before she woke, kicking and screaming?"

This can't be real. Can it?

"Zephyr?"

The man that stood before her squinted his eyes and took a step back. "No ma'am, I'm Theo, and this is Elijah." He shuffled his feet and stepped a little in front of Elijah hiding him from view. "I apologize for disturbing you." He cleared his throat. "Um, I'm not sure... we were told you may be able to help us, may we come in?" His voice wavered with uncertainty.

Téa dropped to her knees, her heart squeezing tight in her chest, the air left her lungs.

He doesn't remember me.

"Ma'am are you alright?" Theo reached for Téa, but stopped short of touching her, and

crouched down. "Is anyone else home? Can I get someone to help you?"

Téa shook her head. "No." She paused.

What if he's here to kill me, maybe he's what Annabelle was trying to warn me about.

"I mean, no, I'm not alone, I have extra security guards in the back of the house." She said, lying. She narrowed her eyes, gathered herself, and stood firmly to her feet.

What am I thinking? It's Zephyr. Even if he doesn't remember me, he would never hurt me. Pull yourself together girl!

Téa plastered a smile on her face. "Please, come inside."

She moved out of the way to allow Zephyr and the boy to pass. Once they were through the door, she shut it tight and turned to face Zephyr, *her Zephyr.* She held back the tears that wanted to flow, her voice shaky. "Now, Theo, you said it was? How can I help you?"

Zephyr wrung his hands and looked around the foyer. "Um, it's kind of a long story." He dropped his hands to his sides and let out a long breath. "We've come here to North Carolina, all the way from western Nebraska. It's been a... difficult journey." He coughed and shuffled his feet again.

"I'm sure this all must seem very odd to you, but perhaps you may know of a place for me and Elijah here," he patted the boy on his back, "to stay for the night?"

In any normal situation, Téa knew she would never have allowed the two to even pass through the threshold of the castle, let alone spend the night. She would have happily suggested nearby lodgings, perhaps even given them some money and sent them on their way. But this was no ordinary circumstance, and he was no ordinary person. It was Zephyr, *her* Zephyr. She didn't keep the General's security, not only because she wanted Sandstone to feel more like a home, but also because she still had her Connex abilities, she could defend herself and her daughter if need be. *Celia.* Her... *their*, precious child.

Téa relaxed and smiled. "Of course. As a matter of fact, I do know a place where you can stay for the night. You can stay here. We have more than enough space. I would be happy to host you and Elijah for the night." She bent down to make eye contact with Elijah. "Are you two hungry? Would you like something to eat before I show you to your rooms?"

Téa stood back up and watched Theo as his expression changed to shock.

I guess he thought I'd recommend a hotel, he probably didn't expect me to invite him to stay here, especially so easily.

Elijah stayed silent and hid behind Theo again. Theo nodded his head. "Um, yes, please that would be great."

Téa brushed her silk pajamas with her hands. "Great! Follow me, the kitchen is this way."

Oh my God. Oh my God. Oh my God. What is happening?

Téa's mind raced. Shock, sadness, then elation, followed by confusion, all flooded through her.

Just keep it together. Let them rest, then figure things out in the morning.

When they reached the kitchen Téa gestured to the stools at the kitchen island. "Here, take a seat. I'll make you both a plate." She went to the fridge and started to rummage through it, speaking with her back to them. "Are leftover chicken tenders and green beans, okay?" She stood, closed the fridge, and faced them as she pulled the lid off the containers in her hands. The pair appeared frozen with surprise, as if she had just offered them a gourmet three course meal.

After a moment, Theo helped Elijah to sit down and leaned the boy's crutches against the kitchen island. Clearing his throat, he said. "That sounds great, thank you." Then sat next to Elijah.

Téa busied herself pulling down plates and grabbed some silverware. "I'm sorry I haven't even introduced myself." She paused, turned, and reached her hand over the kitchen island to Theo. "I'm Téa."

Téa could have sworn she saw Zephyr turn a shade of gray, as though the blood drained from his body. He cleared his throat again and took her offered hand to shake. "Nice to meet you Téa, thank you so much," he paused and dropped her hand, "for everything."

Téa smiled and turned back around to the counter. She spooned food onto the plates and popped them into the microwave. "So, can you tell me anything about yourself, like why you're here?"

Zephyr shifted uncomfortably on his seat. "Um, well, the 'why' is a little... complex. Maybe that's a conversation for the morning-but we don't mean you any harm."

Téa laughed. *Why are you laughing?* She cleared her throat. "Sorry, go on."

Zephyr narrowed his gaze and straightened his shoulders. "As far as about myself, I've been an employee on Elijah's family farm for almost as long as I can remember."

Téa's stomach dropped, and she felt bile rise in her throat, *maybe it's not him.*

Zephyr relaxed. "The truth is, I don't remember anything before about a year ago. I woke in a hospital with neck trauma and no memory." He raised his head a little for Téa to catch of glimpse of a gnarly scar running the length of his neck and solidifying what she knew to be true. This was Zephyr. He continued to talk. "A social worker at the hospital found the job for me, and the rest... is well, for the morning."

Butterflies flew through her, dusting off the love and passion that had fallen asleep inside her. Zephyr, her Zephyr was alive.

I knew it was him!

The microwave beeped. Téa turned away, heart racing, a tear slid down her cheek. She grabbed a hand towel, dabbed her eyes, and pulled their hot plates out, then set them in front of her guests.

Zephyr smiled and nodded. "Thank you, Téa."

Téa's stomach did a somersault at the sound of her name on his lips. "You're very welcome, my pleasure." She smiled.

Zephyr swallowed a bite, then asked. "So do you always invite strangers into your home so easily?" He grinned.

Ah, that grin. She melted.

Téa laughed. "No. But perhaps that is also a story that should wait until morning."

Téa let the gorgeous man, and adorable boy, finish eating without further questions. They wolfed their dinners down in a matter of minutes. When Elijah lifted his plate to start licking it, Téa chuckled. "When was the last time you two had a meal?"

Elijah perked up, his previous shyness ebbed away, and a carefree optimism kicked in. "Food like this? Never! Do you have any more?"

Téa's face fell. She remembered her days at the military base eating imitation food. Her heart sank at the thought of this boy, Celia, or any child ever going hungry. "Of course, little man, you can have as much as you'd like." She tousled his hair.

 Elijah grinned ear to ear. "Hey that's what Theo calls me!" The boy eased from under Téa's hand. "He's always messing with my hair too." He rolled his eyes.

Téa laughed as she looked at Theo, his cheeks were bright red, and she could swear her heart was going to jump from her chest.

After Elijah had his fill, Téa led the pair to their rooms, which were a floor below hers and Celia's. "If either of you needs anything, this intercom system can page me." She pointed to the box next to the door on the wall. "This button here is for my room."

Theo nodded. "Thank you Téa, I really appreciate this."

Téa grasped Zephyr's hand gently. "Truly, it's my pleasure." She hesitated to drop his hand, so warm and familiar, but reluctantly let go and blushed. "Goodnight." She said.

"Goodnight, Téa." He replied.

She hurried away down the hall before he could see the tears spilling out of her.

How could he not remember me?

When Téa arrived at her floor, she quickly checked on Celia. She watched the steady rise and fall of her baby's chest, she slept so peacefully. Téa softly closed the door, then crept to her room. Once inside she shut her door and began to pace.

How can I tell him everything? Where do I start? What if he never wanted children? No. Come on Téa, we talked about starting a family when we thought we were safe at the Sanctuary. What if he changed his mind about kids? How is he here? Why is he here? I need more time with him. I need to leave Angie and William a note.

She quickly wrote a letter to Angie and William, telling them to take the morning off. She was aware of how much they enjoyed morning hikes, and she took a mental note that they hadn't been on one since Eleanor had gone on her trip. Téa hurried to their room, making her way through the dark inner maze of Sandstone estate. Once she was outside their bedroom door, she slipped the note underneath. They always woke with the sun. She knew it would be well before Zephyr and Elijah would be up since it was so late already. Téa knew Angie and William would be gone all day. This would leave her plenty of time to talk things through with Zephyr tomorrow.

On the way back to her room, she resisted the urge to go check on Zephyr and make sure he was still there. *Maybe I've had a mental break, maybe I'm hallucinating... No... I never could have imagined a kid as cute as Elijah.*

She forced herself not to stop until she got back to her room. She checked the time, 2:45 a.m. Then ensured the baby monitor was still turned up all the way, and reluctantly crawled into bed.

Chapter Ten
Theo

Moonlight streamed through the window. Theo lay on his back in the grand bed unable to fall asleep despite his bones aching, and his eyelids like two weights pulling down from his lashes. The journey had been long, but his mind raced.

She definitely recognized me. I wonder if she knows who I am? Maybe she has answers. And her name... when she introduced herself, I could have sworn that name had fallen from my lips before, Téa, exactly as Elijah had said.

Theo shivered despite the comfortable temperature in the room. He rolled to lay on his side.

What am I going to tell her tomorrow?

'Oh yeah, a meteor hit our house and some lady that only Elijah could hear was talking to him through the radio, she told us to come, that's why we're here.'

She'll definitely throw us out, then what? Where will we go? What am I going to do with Elijah?

Theo groaned and sat up. "I need sleep." Yet despite his needs, he stood up and decided to take a walk along the hallway outside his room, maybe it would quiet his mind.

No sooner had he left his room, he heard a shrill scream from the room next door.

Elijah.

Theo raced towards it and flung the door open. The boy was sitting in his bed crying.

"Hey..." Theo crossed the room in two steps, sat on the edge of the bed, and rubbed Elijah's back. "Hey little man, are you okay?"

Elijah looked up with his big eyes shimmering with tears. "I want mama, Theo." The boy began a new wave of sobs.

What do I do?

Theo moved his hand in slow circles on Elijah's back. "I hear you, little man. I hear you. I miss them too kiddo."

Elijah raised his little head and wiped his nose on his sleeve. "You do?"

Theo straightened and looked at Elijah. "Of course I do, your mom and dad were the greatest people I've ever known!" He paused and smiled. "And you know what else." Theo leaned closer and whispered. "You carry them in your heart, right here." He pointed to Elijah's chest. "Always."

Elijah's tears slowed and he sniffled. "Really?"

"Most definitely." He said, brow knitted together in serious reflection. "You are a part of them, and they are a part of you. As long as we remember the loved ones we've lost, they'll live forever."

Elijah smiled. "Like Annabelle?"

Theo tilted his head. "What do you mean?"

"The lady in the radio. Remember?" Theo's blood ran cold, and Elijah continued. "Annabelle said that Téa still has her powers because she has a little bit of Annabelle's soul with her. It's just like Ma and Pa, I have a piece of their heart!"

Jesus, Mary, and Joseph!

Theo put on a brave face for the sake of the kid, despite the fear chilling his bones. "Exactly, just like Annabelle, you keep your mom and dad in your heart."

Elijah smiled. "Theo?"

"Yeah, little man?"

"Will you stay in here tonight?"

Theo panicked.

What's the protocol for this?

"Yeah, kiddo, sure. Let me just go get a blanket and pillow, I'll sleep right here on the floor, okay?

"Okay, Theo."

Theo went back out into the hall and closed the door behind him.

What are we going to do?

Inside his room, he grabbed a blanket and pillow, then went back to Elijah's room. He fidgeted as he tried to get comfortable on the floor.

"Goodnight, kiddo."

"Goodnight, Theo."

It'll be okay, we'll figure everything out in the morning.

The next morning Theo and Elijah woke to a note that was slid under the door.

Elijah tried to peer around Theo's shoulder. "What's that Theo?"

Theo turned to face Elijah. "It's a map, it says, 'See you at breakfast X marks the spot'. It shows us how to get back to the kitchen. Apparently, this place is pretty big." He said with a wink.

Elijah grabbed his elbow crutches and walked over to Theo. "It's like an adventure! Just like Dr. Symbico vs. Sir Festivus! See Theo? We're supposed to be here, Téa is fun!"

Theo smiled. "All right little man, well, are you hungry?"

Elijah was practically vibrating with excitement. "Yes! I'm starving, Theo! Let's go!"

As they arrived at the kitchen, a warm, delectable-smelling steam settled over Theo. Téa was moving around the kitchen like a well-choreographed dance. Mixing one bowl, turning something over in a pan, checking inside the oven. Moving with the experience of a seasoned chef, nothing like he'd seen from Gertrude on the farm.

He cleared his throat. "Good morning."

A warmth spread through Theo's body as she turned to face him. "Good morning you two! Did you sleep well? Did you find the kitchen okay? Are you hungry?"

Theo's head swam with all the questions, she barely paused to take a breath.

Elijah piped up. "We're starving!"

Theo's knees became weak at the sound of Téa's laughter.

What's happening to me?

He moved to help Elijah sit down before taking his own seat. His eyes could not pull away from this woman fluttering around the kitchen.

Those eyes, the curl of her hair-the way it fell gracefully across her neck and shoulders. Get a grip, Theo.

After a few minutes Téa placed full plates of food in front of him and Elijah, filled with scrambled eggs, bacon, a blueberry muffin, and a glass of milk.

After he had taken a few bites, Téa spoke up as she leaned on the kitchen island across from them. "So, we sure do have a lot to talk about, don't we?"

Theo swallowed his bite of food and took a drink before responding. "I suppose we do."

How do I tell her the kid talks to a lady in the radio?

"But maybe we can finish breakfast first? And then maybe Elijah here could take a tour of the castle while we talk?"

Kid could use a nice distraction.

Theo watched as color flooded Téa's cheeks, she stood straight and smiled. "Most definitely. That's a great idea. I bet Elijah would love to check out the library." She winked at Elijah.

Theo could not stop staring.

That smile.

Elijah snapped to attention. "Do you have any comic books?'

Téa laughed. "I think we do actually, have you ever heard of Dr. Symbico vs. Sir Festivus?"

Elijah bounced in his chair. "Oh my gosh, Theo! Can you believe it!?"

Téa turned to look at Theo, and he froze. His heart suspended in the beauty of the moment.

"I take it Elijah is a fan?" She asked.

Theo gulped. "Yes, that would be an understatement." He chuckled.

Elijah practically swallowed his food whole in an effort to finish quickly. When they were all done eating, Téa led them to the library and showed Elijah the comics. Across the library from Elijah, Theo and Téa sat on a red velvet couch. Theo watched as she took what looked like a radio that was clipped to her back pocket and set it on the coffee table in front of them with a soft thud.

She turned to face him. "Do you want to go first?"

Theo rubbed his hands down the tops of his legs and started to pump one leg up and down. "I'm not sure where to start."

Téa gently placed a hand on his leg, stilling his nerves, and he thought his heart might jump out of his chest.

She said. "Why don't you start at the beginning?"

Theo took a deep breath and let it out slowly. Then he proceeded to tell her everything. From waking up in the hospital with no memory, to working on the farm, the meteor, and even Elijah, and what he heard through the radio.

Téa stared at him, she looked frozen, then said. "Elijah told you that? That I had a piece of Annabelle's soul? That's why I still have some Connex-A powers?"

Theo laughed. "That's your biggest question? The most impossible part and you're asking a question about it as though you have no doubt in the world that it's real?"

Téa's brow furrowed, and she shifted her body towards him. "Yes. Because Annabelle was my sister, my soulmate. There's no way Elijah could have known that. And even though they are not as strong as they once were, I do have Connex-A abilities. She paused before continuing. "I also have Connex-B abilities that are full strength."

Theo heard his blood pounding in his ears as though amplified by a speaker and heating his body. "You have abilities?"

"Yes."

His vision blurred everything around him, except this woman sitting next to him. "And what about you, Téa? What's your story? What do you know about me-and don't try to deny it, I can tell you recognize me."

She pulled her hand away from his leg, and he started pumping it up and down again. He moved his hand to his mouth and started chewing on his nails. Téa pulled his hand away from his teeth gently cupping his hands within hers and spoke calmly. "I do know you. And you knew me."

"How?"

She hesitated before answering. "Your name is, Zephyr. You were the son of General Thomas Strauss. You and I were matched to be married. You grew up here, at Sandstone Estate."

Theo pulled his hand away from hers and stood quickly. "That's impossible, how could I not remember something that huge? There's no way!"

Téa stood beside him and placed a hand on his shoulder. "Zephyr, how did you find your way here? How did you know how to get to Sandstone? Sure, most people know the general location, but the exact spot? That's not on any map."

He stilled and his stomach dropped. "I... I don't know. I just started driving."

Téa stepped in front of him and looked him straight in the eyes.

Oh God, those eyes.

"Somewhere, deep inside, you knew how to come home. You knew how to get back to me."

Theo shook his head. "A wife? How could I not remember having a wife!?"

Téa looked away from him before answering. "We were just matched; we never got the chance to be married." She turned around and took a step away from him. "A lot happened in a very short amount of time. There's a lot I need to tell you."

Theo felt a pull in his core, telling him to wrap his arms around her. He fought his instincts but did gently grab her shoulder to turn her back around to face him. She had tears streaming down her beautiful face.

I want to kiss those tears away.

Téa shuddered before she spoke. "There is so much to say Zephyr, but the most important part is..."

Theo could listen to that voice for hours, *those lips.*

She continued. "You-we, have a daughter, her name is Celia."

He froze, his eyes widened, the air knocked out of him. "I have a daughter?"

As if on cue, the radio Téa had sat on the table lit up and a baby's cry sounded from it.

Téa reached for it before answering. "Yes, we do."

Chapter Eleven

Téa

Téa left the library in a hurry to get to Celia. As she walked the long quiet hallways, she chided herself.

What was I expecting? Him to be overjoyed at finding out he had a daughter? Of course, he's in shock, give him a break Téa!

She swiped away her angry tears.

He didn't seem thrilled, but he also didn't seem... unhappy? The point is, he's alive, and he's home.

That thought gave her a small amount of hope that Zephyr could come back to her. She had arrived at Celia's bedroom door and shook off her emotions, rotated her shoulders in circles, and stomped her feet to get some feeling and warmth back in her toes. She didn't want her daughter to sense any negativity coming from her mother, so she did her best to shake it off.

The door squeaked as she opened it. She walked in and softly cooed. "Hi baby girl, mommy's here." She reached for Celia and cuddled her crying baby to her chest. "Shhh, shh, sh. I'm here now."

She sat in the soft blue rocking chair and nursed her daughter; then patted her back when she was finished eating, and Celia let out a burp that could rival any grown man. Téa laughed and placed her back in the crib. Then grabbed a piece of long stretchy fabric and began wrapping it around herself creating a kangaroo-type pouch on her front. She picked Celia back up and took her to the changing table for a new diaper. Praying Celia had enough time after eating to do her business, her daughter had a knack of waiting for a new diaper before soiling herself. "Okay my strong, beautiful, independent girl, are you ready to meet your daddy?"

Téa's jaw clenched, and she made a sign of the cross. Gabriela from the Sanctuary had started teaching Téa prayer and how to use a rosary when Téa found out she was pregnant. Téa hoped there was a God, somewhere out there, that would protect them from harm. She didn't know if she believed in Gabriela's God, but Téa believed there was something, or someone, out there in the universe bigger than themselves.

She trusted Gabriela and figured learning her Catholic faith would at the very least provide a greater understanding of Téa's mother, may she rest in peace. Eleanor kept rosary beads that had belonged to Téa's mom and gave them to Téa after Celia's birth. The rosary had become an effective calming technique for Téa, whether or not she believed in them. She would rub the cool smooth beads between her fingers and talk to the mother she craved to know. Wishing for advice, wisdom, and strength. Currently, it rested on a dresser in Celia's room. She grabbed the rosary and tucked it in one of the pockets of her flowy yellow summer dress. Téa picked Celia back up, and carefully strapped her baby into the wrap, close to her heart. "Let's do this."

As she walked back to the library her heart began to race. Téa patted Celia's bum and rubbed her back while making small adjustments to the baby carrier, ensuring it was tightly secure around her daughter.

When she arrived at the hallway that led to the library, she paused and took a deep breath. The gleaming white floors with flakes of gold dust shone in the sunlight pouring in from the wall of windows lining one side. Téa's steps echoed with each movement. When she reached the massive ornate library doors with opal inlays, she placed her palm on them and took another deep breath. *You've got this.* She pushed the doors open and walked through.

The forced smile that spread across her face became genuine the moment she laid eyes on Zephyr. Happiness reached her eyes and warmed her heart. He was pacing and chewing his cuticles. Elijah was still over in the corner enthralled by the comic books. Téa slowly made her way towards Zephyr, as though he were an anxious cat ready to race across the room.

He appeared deep in thought and hadn't noticed her approach, so she gently ran her hand up the side of his arm and cleared her throat. "Zephyr?" He was startled at the sound of her voice before she continued. "I'm sorry, would you prefer Theo?"

He shook his head and dropped his hands to his sides before stuffing them in his pockets, "Honestly, I'm not sure. I haven't been Theo for all that long really, but it's all I can remember, but if you're saying I'm this Zephyr guy, I suppose I should try and get used to that name." He shrugged his shoulders and let out a deep breath. "This is surreal." He sat back down on the red velvet couch and put his head in his hands, then peeked through his fingers. He stared at Celia and stood back up with a huge grin spreading ear to ear. "Is this?... Is this my-our daughter?"

Téa let out a breath of relief. "Yes, this is Celia." She grinned and gently pulled Celia from the baby wrap. "Would you like to hold her?"

Zephyr radiated warmth and his smile illuminated the room, he nodded. Téa carefully supported Celia's head and body as she passed her baby girl into her father's waiting arms. Téa's heart thumped out a jazz number, and her legs and arms tingled, her whole body electrified with a hope she thought she would never feel again. Watching Zephyr sway side to side and smiling at their daughter was an image that would never be undone in her mind's eye.

Zephyr looked up from the baby in his arms and locked eyes with Téa. "She's beautiful."

Téa could not hold back the happy tears that spilled from the corner of her eyes. "Yeah, she really is." She let out a soft laugh, looked down, and softly stroked the side of Celia's face. "I didn't get rid of your things. They're all neatly packed in the attic above my-I mean your, room. There are also so many things from your childhood. I saved everything. Would you like to hold Celia for a while, and I'll see if I can find you and Elijah some clean clothes?"

Zephyr tensed. "Ah, are you sure? What if she cries?"

Téa laughed. "I'm sure you'll be okay. She just ate and I gave her a new diaper. If she cries just walk around and sing to her." Téa smiled and gave Zephyr a reassuring pat on the back. "I'll be quick, I promise."

Zephyr gave Téa a meek smile and shaky nod. "Okay, we'll be here."

Téa laughed again as she left the library floating on a wave of joy that felt like it could never be dimmed again.

When she reached the attic above her room, a thin layer of dust tickled her nose and she sneezed. The room was dimly lit from a half oval window that was tall enough for her to stand in. The wooden floorboards creaked as she made her way to the wall of boxes lining one side of the room. She packed every item herself, with the exception of the General's belongings, which she burned to ash. But had refused to let go of anything belonging to Zephyr. Téa had organized well, everything carefully cataloged. She had spent countless hours poring over old photographs, breathing in the scent of his clothes, spraying her pillow in his cologne, and sleeping in his sheets. Opening the boxes as she searched for clothing for both Elijah and Zephyr was like releasing old ghosts that had a hold on her heart. Each opened flap was another painful scar being healed.

Téa grabbed the clothing that she needed and filled an empty box with multiple changes of clothes. Then found a photo album from Zephyr's childhood that she planned on sharing with him later. She was beaming so much her cheeks started to hurt as she made her way back to the library.

Téa balanced the box between her knee and one arm as she opened the door. Upon entering she found Elijah and Zephyr leaning over the baby laughing and making funny faces as Celia cooed and kicked her legs in delight on the floor. Téa thought her heart might explode.

She quietly set the box down and sat on the floor next to Zephyr. "I see things are going well here."

When Zephyr sat up on his legs from leaning over Celia and looked at Téa, her stomach did a somersault. He grinned. "Very well, she's perfect."

Surely, he could hear her heart singing, blaring. Téa cleared her throat. "Um, so I found the clothes, and a photo album you might want to see. I was thinking I can make everyone some lunch while you and Elijah change, then we could look at the pictures together?"

Zephyr paled a little and his smile faltered for just a moment, then he nodded. "That sounds great. Hey Elijah buddy, we've got some new clothes little man, let's go get cleaned up." He helped Elijah to his feet and passed him his crutches.

Zephyr

As Elijah and Zephyr made their way back to their separate rooms Zephyr's heart raced. The thought of looking at pictures from a life he couldn't remember was unnerving him for reasons he could not explain. But then he thought of Celia. That sheer goodness that came from that perfect little being, was enough to chase away any gnawing fears.

He looked to Elijah. "Hey buddy, so I saw each of our showers are pretty huge, they have seats to sit down and everything. Do you think you'll be okay on your own?"

Elijah scoffed and rolled his eyes. "Duh Theo, I'm not a baby."

He laughed and patted him on the back. "You're right little man, you're not a baby. So, I'll meet you in the hallway when you're ready?"

Elijah stopped. "Why? Are you scared to walk to the kitchen alone Theo?" He grinned, then kept walking. "Last one there is a rotten egg!" He shouted as he entered his room and slammed the door.

Zephyr chuckled to himself.

Nice to have him back to his old self.

When Zephyr arrived at the kitchen freshly showered and rejuvenated. He found Elijah devouring a sandwich with dripping wet hair. He laughed to himself. "You win little man, but maybe next time at least attempt to dry off." Elijah tried to talk with his mouth full and instead waved Zephyr off.

Zephyr chuckled and took a seat. When Téa put a full plate of food in front of him and saw Celia wrapped close to her mother's chest, his heart began to race. "Thank you," he said.

She smiled. "You're welcome" then sat next to him. He had the urge to wrap an arm around her shoulders but resisted and took a bite of potato salad instead.

Zephyr didn't know what to say and was grateful for Elijah who was asking question after question. 'How big is Sandstone?' 'How many rooms does it have?' 'Will you get new comics?' 'Do you have a swimming pool?' 'I have read about swimming pools.' 'I bet I'd be the best swimmer in the whole world.' On and on until everyone was finished eating.

He offered to help when Téa started to clear the table, but she waved him away. When she finished, she asked. "Would you like to take a walk outside?"

"Yeah, that sounds great." He said.

Zephyr's body tensed, and he clenched his jaw as they made their way towards a bench outside. Téa had a blanket under her arms and laid it out on the grass in front of them. She placed Celia carefully on the blanket and put a baby toy gently in her hand that crinkled as she grasped it.

Zephyr hollered at Elijah as the boy wandered further down a gravel path that led into a garden. "Don't go too far kiddo!"

Elijah waved a hand behind him as he kept walking.

Téa sat down on the bench with the photo album in her lap, and Zephyr sat next to her. She passed him the book. He took a deep breath and opened the first page. His hands shook, and he gripped the album tighter. This was his life. He was going to find out, finally, who he was. Warmth spread up his sides as he flipped through the pages. It was all photos of him and a beautiful young woman, who Téa said was his mother. He willed his memories to come back to him as he stared at the smiling faces, but there was nothing.

The last picture was a stiff and formal family photo of himself as a teenager, his mother, and a man who Téa said was the General. Téa took his hand before she spoke. "This is the only photo of the General, I was tempted to burn it with the rest of his belongings, but it's the last photo of your mother, and I didn't have the heart to destroy it." She took a deep breath before she continued. "This is the man who tried to kill you."

Zephyr's blood ran cold, he pulled his hand from Téa's and closed his eyes. He tried to push down the roar that was building inside of him when a shrill scream came from the gardens. Zephyr jumped up and ran towards the sound. His heart raced as fast as his feet. Zephyr sprinted through the garden towards Elijah. He skidded to a halt scattering gravel as he looked at Elijah curled up on the ground squeezing his hands over his ears.

He kneeled down next to him, shaking his shoulders. "Elijah! Elijah! What's wrong? What happened?" The boy didn't answer and started to cry.

Zephyr heard Téa's pounding feet as she came up behind them. Elijah finally sat up, sniffled, and wiped his nose on his sleeve. His voice was barely a whisper as he looked at Téa and said. "We're all going to die. Annabelle says hurry." Elijah started to cry again and leaned against Zephyr. "We're all going to die Theo."

Zephyr looked at Téa with desperation in his eyes. She sat next to Elijah and rubbed his back. "Hey, it's okay. Everything is going to be okay. No one is going to die."

Elijah wiped his nose again and glared at her. "You don't know that!"

Zephyr's voice was firm but kind. "Hey, take it easy buddy."

Téa placed a hand on Zephyr's shoulder. "It's okay." Then looked back to Elijah. "What happened?"

Elijah sniffled then sat up. "Annabelle showed me the world exploding, then a face. He looked like you Theo, but just a little different. I think we need to find him."

Téa smiled. "Well good news, I know exactly who that is." She looked at Zephyr. "How would you like to meet your brother?"

Chapter Twelve
Zephyr

Zephyr's blood rushed through his veins, excitement mixed with a nervous energy surged through him at the prospect of unlocking another piece of his life. "Brother? I have a brother?"

Téa smiled at him. "Yes, and he's amazing."

Zephyr's voice ticked up a notch in pitch. "Maybe he'll be able to help answer some more questions for me, maybe I have a chance at remembering my life, who better than a brother with a shared childhood!"

Téa's face dropped, her eyes stared at the dirt beneath her shoes. "I'm so sorry Zephyr, but you didn't know about him, before. He doesn't actually know more about you than I did. It's a long story."

Zephyr's heart sank in his chest, and a new wave of sorrow and disappointment flooded through him. He didn't want Téa to feel sorry for him though, so he was trying to think of something positive to say when suddenly she sprung up from where she was kneeling next to Elijah and shouted over her shoulder. "I left Celia on the blanket!"

Zephyr was torn between chasing after her or staying with Elijah. He decided to stay and help Elijah to his feet. The castle was surrounded by hundreds of acres, no one around for miles. Celia would be fine, she wasn't even rolling over yet from what he could tell, the worst thing that could happen was a bug crawling on her, he thought to himself.

"Come on buddy, let's get you up." Zephyr pulled Elijah to his feet when he heard a scream in the distance. His stomach shot up to his throat as panic seized him. "Elijah, kiddo why don't you wait here buddy while I go see what's going on, okay?"

Without waiting for an answer, Zephyr raced back towards Téa, he could hear her shouting Celia's name. He skidded to a halt. "What's going on?"

Téa's eyes were searching, she paced, her breathing ragged, her face transformed to that of a wild animal, a lioness looking for her cub. "I don't know, I left Celia right here on the blanket, right here, and she's gone! Maybe Angie and William are back from their hike, maybe they brought her inside."

Her words flowed out so quickly it was hard for him to process it all. "Wait, who are Angie and William?" But Téa was already running back inside the castle.

When it sunk in what Téa was saying, he debated again, he couldn't leave Elijah behind if something evil was lurking in the shadows. He hurried back to where he left Elijah in the gardens. When he got there it was nothing but an empty space.

Zephyr swayed on his feet, his hand searching for something to hold on to. He pressed one palm to his temple as the sky switched places with the ground, the world swirling around him.

He screamed to the open air. "ELIJAH!" He turned in circles and scanned the horizon, nothing but greenery and flowers blocked his view. "ELIJAH!" He sprinted back towards the castle. Zephyr tried to force oxygen into his lungs, his breathing came in gasps. He charged in through the open back door that led into the kitchen, to find Téa yelling as an older couple listened who looked as shocked as he felt.

"You didn't see anything!? How can a baby just disappear!? She has to be here! She has to be." As Téa's screams turned into sobs she fell to the marble floor, her knees hitting the ground with a soft thud as she covered her face with her hands and started to cry uncontrollably.

Zephyr tried to talk, but his voice would not come. He cleared his throat and tried again. "Elijah is gone too."

The older woman standing next to the older man looked up at him and dropped the water bottle she was holding. She grabbed her mouth with one hand, her eyes wide. She took a tentative step forward before slowly collapsing. The older man caught her before her head hit the ground then looked at Zephyr. His face flushed red and his surprise quickly turned to anger. "You! You had something to do with this! Where's Celia? What did you do!?"

Zephyr raised his arms in defense. "I had nothing to do with this!" He screeched. "My boy is missing too!"

The old man stared incredulously at him. "Your boy? You have no children." He glared.

How could this man know that? Does he know who I am too?

Téa shook her head and stood up quickly. "Enough! Both of you!" She looked at Zephyr, concern creasing her features. "Elijah is gone too?" Zephyr nodded his head and Téa continued, "They can't be far, they were just here, everyone spread out and start searching as fast as you can!"

The old man looked torn. "I'm sorry Téa, I can't leave Angie like this, I'll call for help."

Téa's eyes welled with tears. "Please William, it's my baby, my baby girl." her shoulders started to shake.

William stood, straightened his back, and looked down at Téa. "My darling girl, I understand, I do. But it will do no one any good to run around in a frenzy." Téa wiped her nose on the back of her hand and nodded, then William continued to speak. "It seems as though whoever took these children has been watching us for some time, I highly doubt they left on foot. I'll call for help. You take Zephyr to the garage, one of you head to the north gate, and the other to the southern gate. Take radios, switch them to channel four, I have one here on the same channel."

Without another word Téa started to run back out of the kitchen door, she paused for a brief moment to look behind her. "Zephyr! Are you coming!?"

Zephyr nodded and turned to follow her. "Lead the way."

They raced towards the garage, Zephyr searched all around them as they ran, ready and willing to attack, hoping for someone to show their face. They reached the massive square concrete structure and Téa swung open the heavy metal door. He followed her to a wall of supplies where dozens of walkie-talkies sat. She grabbed one and turned it on. She was about to turn the dial to channel four when a thick masculine voice oozed out of the small black thing.

'Hello... heeelloooo... I can see you...I know you can hear me. If you want your children back you will do exactly as I say.'

Zephyr stiffened and yanked the walkie-talkie from Téa's hand, she glared at him as he spoke into the device. "Who the fuck is this!?" he shouted.

Téa grabbed his arm, pulling the walkie-talkie away from his mouth. "Zephyr, calm down, *now*. They have Celia, they have Elijah. We cannot risk *pissing* them off." She paused before continuing. "And don't ever yank anything out of my hand like that again, got it?"

Acrid bile rose in his throat, and he nodded before speaking. "You're right, I'm sorry... I'm just...I'm just scared."

She placed a hand on his forearm and heat tingled up his arm, speaking more softly this time, she said. "I know, I'm scared too, but we have to keep our heads straight, for them."

Zephyr swallowed, and the voice crept out of the device again, sending a chill up his spine. 'Now, now, is that any way to speak?' The voice on the walkie-talkie said, and a baby's cry carried to his ears from behind the sound of the man's voice. Zephyr's blood ran cold. Téa clenched her fists and shook beside him, craning her neck as though she could see Celia through the walkie-talkie.

The voice spoke to them again. "We have been watching you for months now. You will travel to the sanctuary. You will meet us in the mines leading into the front entrance. You have twenty-four hours. Do you understand?"

Zephyr's throat had gone dry again, his jaw stuck together. Téa took the walkie-talkie from him and replied. "Yes, we understand. Please don't' hurt our children. Wait, wait, please, Celia, she needs to eat every 2-3 hours, and she'll get a diaper rash if you don't change her often..."

She was still pleading with the person on the other end when the line went quiet. Zephyr's heart cracked as he watched Téa fall to the floor weeping. He sat beside her and wrapped his arms around her, running his fingers through her curls.

She sniffled and looked up into his eyes and he thought his heart might stop beating when she whispered. "We have to leave right now." He gulped. "Whoever took them, they must have some kind of teleportation ability, to grab the kids as fast as they did and disappear without a trace." She paused for air. "Zephyr, it's a twenty-three-hour drive and the forest gets really thick, we'll have to walk the last mile or so, we only have one extra hour, what if we run into problems, a flat tire, who knows, we need to go now."

Zephyr could feel her panic rising, every molecule in his body was screaming at him to make everything better, for her. To comfort her. He gently cupped her chin with his hand, took a deep breath, and placed his lips on hers. Electricity flowed through him, and she softened at his touch. He could taste the salt from her tears on his lips. When he pulled away, he looked in her eyes. "We'll get them back, Téa, I promise."

She wrapped herself closer to his chest, and he breathed in the scent of lilac in her hair, before carefully pulling her to stand with him. "Let's go tell William what's happened, grab some food and water, and then we'll go."

Téa nodded and leaned her head against his shoulder. "You know, William and Angie were the kitchen staff when you and your father lived here. Now they still do most of the cooking, but they are more like family to me. They've known you since birth, if you want answers about your childhood later, they'll have them." Zephyr's heart raced as she paused, then kept talking. "I'm so sorry Zephyr, I just wanted some time with you by myself, so I sent them on a hike this morning. I shouldn't have done that. You deserved the chance to talk with them."

He gently tugged her towards the door, gesturing that they should start hurrying back to the castle. "Hey, it's okay, I understand." He grinned. "I'd want time alone with me too." He winked, an attempt to break the tension and ease their fear, the same that Téa must be doing by changing the topic of conversation, but it all felt... wrong. Their kids were in the hands of a stranger, a powerful one at that to have been watching them and taken them so easily.

Téa smiled weakly and grasped his hand before her face fell again. "What if they hurt them, Zephyr? Or don't feed Celia, what if they don't have formula, it's hard to find these days? Or what if they try to give her water? Or normal milk instead of formula?"

They walked outside to a cool breeze that rustled his hair and sent a chill down his spine. Zephyr stopped. He gripped her by the arms and said with an intensity he didn't know that he had inside of him. "I swear on my life, Téa, I will do everything in my power to bring our daughter, and Elijah home."

"Zephyr, don't you dare." Her voice hitched. "Don't swear anything on your life. Please. I can't go through that again." She took a deep breath. "We'll get them back, together." Zephyr let go of her, and when she caressed the side of his arm and squeezed his hand, he knew, somehow, that he had finally found the place that he belonged. It was with her. He didn't know what would happen next, but he knew as long as he was by her side, he could survive anything that came next.

Chapter Thirteen

Téa

They ran through the gardens as fast as their legs could carry them. A bee buzzed in Téa's ear as she and Zephyr sprinted through its territory, cutting across the flowers, red rose petals sprayed the green ground around them like sprays of blood. They hustled to get back to the kitchens where they had left Angie and William.

Oxygen pushed in and out of her lungs, burning with each gasp of breath. She leaned against the door frame at the back entrance of the castle and shouted through the open doorway. "The kidnappers made contact!"

William, who was still kneeled on the floor where Angie had fallen in the kitchen, lifted his gaze to meet Téa's. "What were their demands? How much are they asking?"

Heavy thuds behind Téa alerted her to Zephyr's arrival, despite her deep anxiety and heartbreak, she couldn't help but feel a small bit of satisfaction that she had finally become the faster runner of the pair.

A sheen of sweat dotted his brow, his own breathing labored, Zephyr replied for her. "They didn't. They didn't demand anything other than a time and place to meet. There wasn't a money ransom."

William furrowed his brow. "Something is off about that."

Téa moved further into the kitchen to allow Zephyr inside as well. She stood at the kitchen island and slammed her fist on the counter. "I don't give a damn! It's my daughter! Suspicious or not, I have to follow through, we only have one extra hour to spare, we have to go now!"

Zephyr gently rubbed Téa's back as a single tear pooled at the top of her nose. He was kind when he spoke. "Hey, it's okay, of course, we're going. Why don't you go pack up anything you might need for Celia, clothing, and a first aid kit. I'll start packing some food and I'm sure William can tell me where I can find some tactical gear. Right, William?" He asked as he nodded towards the old man.

William stuttered, looking at Téa confused. She looked at William. "I'm sorry William, I shouldn't have shouted at you like that." She swallowed the lump in her throat. "If you could help Zephyr, I don't have time to explain, but this *is him*, he's alive, but he has a pretty bad case of amnesia."

William nodded his understanding, then cleared his throat. "Yes, I can help get you packed." Then he looked back to Téa with meaning in his eyes, something like understanding wrapped up in loyalty. "Anything you need."

She wiped her nose on her sleeve, and walked over to the old man, placing her hand gently on his shoulder. "I don't imagine I'll ever be able to thank you enough, but I can try, thank you, William." She hugged him then, as a tear rolled down the man's large hair filled nose, and he nodded.

She looked back to Zephyr. "Fifteen minutes, that's it, and we'll meet back here."

"Got it, fifteen minutes."

Téa swirled on her toes to hurry through the exit of the kitchen when she stopped short and looked down at Angie. "I'm so sorry, William will she be okay?"

The old man rubbed the top of his balding head and dragged his hand over his face. "I believe so. She just faint-ed, you know, from basically seeing a ghost." He looked pointedly at Zephyr and grunted. "The volunteer firefight-ers are the best option we have around here as far as emergency support goes, and when I called, I was informed that they're currently occupied elsewhere." He took a deep breath and continued. "I think I have some smelling salts in the guest bath on the first floor. Would you mind, if you think of it, grabbing them on your way back?"

Téa knelt again next to William and enclosed his hands in hers. "Of course. I'll be right back."

Téa positioned herself behind the steering wheel of a black SUV; Zephyr sat in the passenger seat and rubbed his hands up and down the tops of his legs as they drove. The newly rejuvenated landscape was mostly made up of long-ago abandoned homes that were slowly being consumed by nature. Long thick vines that cemented themselves to crumbling brick walls, trees shooting up from the center of ghost-filled living rooms spreading their branches towards the sun through collapsed roofs. The yellow dashes on the road blurred together as they raced forward on the two-lane black pavement.

Téa didn't know what to say as she drove. Her mind so consumed with thoughts of her daughter. But after about thirty minutes of silence since they had left Sandstone, Zephyr finally spoke first. "We should probably switch places every five hours or so. What do you think?"

Téa nodded. "Sure, that's fine. Can you read a map, is that something you remember? I can mark out our route for you."

Zephyr chuckled. "Yes, I can read a map."

Silence.

Zephyr gulped. "So how familiar are you with this place that we're headed?"

Her jaw clenched and her grip tightened. "Very." She took a deep breath in and let it out slowly. "Or, at least I used to be. It's had some improvements since the last time I was there." She paused again, and stole a glance in his direction. "It was destroyed pretty badly some months ago. Your brother and his wife live there now. But I haven't been back."

Zephyr looked at her sideways and ran his fingers through his hair. "Back? Since it was destroyed? What happened?"

Téa's body trembled at the memory of it. The blood, fire, ashes, and then the rain. "Um, can we talk about something else?"

It seemed like time passed slowly. She could feel his questioning eyes on her body as he marinated on her request. She was grateful when he finally replied. "Of course. Tell me about Angie and William instead? Your dad definitely seemed to hate me." He laughed softly.

Téa snorted. "Oh, William? He's not my father. And he doesn't hate you. He's probably just suspicious of people who are supposed to be dead." She softly chuckled.

"What do you mean by that?"

Her skin was suddenly sensitive to the cool air flowing out of the car vents. "Zephyr, we thought you were dead. You never wondered why no one came looking for you?"

She could see out of the corner of her eye as he dropped his head down and to the side, busying himself by looking out of the window, that she had hit a nerve.

His voice came out faintly. "I've wondered a lot of things. Mostly if there was more for me, somewhere out in the world." He raised his eyes to meet hers. "Being with you, has been the first time I have felt complete. Like I could be happy. I can't explain it, it's just a feeling somewhere deep within me."

Her throat restricted the words from coming out, and her teeth chattered. She dropped one hand from the steering wheel and pierced her fingernails into her palm. Finally, her muscles eased, and a small hiccup escaped her before her shaky voice poured out. "If I had known." Another deep breath. "If I had known that you were alive, Zephyr, I would have found you, anywhere on this planet or the next. I would have found you." She steeled herself, there was no going back now. "Zephyr, I love you. I know there's a lot of missing pieces for you, but I never got a chance to tell you, before. I love you with all that I am."

Zephyr swiped at his face, he let out a shaky breath. "Please, Téa, tell me what happened? How much do you know? When was the last time you saw me?"

She was so overwhelmed with the past flooding to the present, nausea rolled in her gut.

The tires squealed underneath them as Téa slammed on the brakes and pulled to the side of the road. She flung herself out of the vehicle and made it to the ditch before she puked, grateful her long curly locks were tied up into a bun. She squeezed her sides as the contents of her stomach emptied from her.

Zephyr got out of the SUV and brought her a water bottle. Thankful, she spit, then took a long pull of the refreshing liquid, swished it around in her mouth, and spit again.

They walked back to the SUV, she leaned against the front, and squinting at him said. "I can't keep driving while we talk about this, and I don't think it would be safe for you to drive while hearing it. So, I'm going to say this quickly, and once we've gotten our children back, I'll answer every and any question you have, Zephyr, I promise."

He stood staring at her with his arms crossed and leaned next to her on the hood of the car. "Fair enough."

Téa took another deep breath and looked at the sky, she couldn't bear to meet his gaze as she recounted their final moments together. When she finished, he wouldn't look at her. She watched as he walked a few feet away, then bent over with his hands on his knees, shoulders shaking. Téa hurried over to him and wrapped her arms around his back. He straightened, turned into her embrace, and cried into her chest. Her heart broke for him all over again.

They drove in silence for a long while after that. Neither knew what to say to the other. The heat of the day slowly cooled into night. The twilight dazzled them with brilliant hues of orange, yellow, red, and purple until night finally overtook them. Glittering stars wrapped them into a false embrace of comfort as they drove across the country. The hum and vibrations of the road lulled Téa into a deep sleep as Zephyr took his turn driving.

The bright early rays of sunlight pierced her closed eyes. She yawned and stretched as much as she could. Her joints ached and her back was stiff. They must be getting close. Téa looked around their surroundings before speaking. "Zephyr, it's time to switch. You need some rest before we get there."

He nodded and pulled to the side of the road. Téa got back into the driver's seat and continued on their way. With Zephyr fast asleep, the darkness of fear started to overtake her again. Thinking of every worst-case scenario, she pressed the gas further, willing the car to move faster. She cursed the heavens, wishing she still had full strength Connex-A powers to be able to teleport them there. The drive felt too long, and too slow.

Her breasts ached and when she looked down, she saw that her shirt was wet. She hadn't nursed her daughter or pumped in nearly twenty hours. Téa held back the tears that wanted to overflow and focused on her driving. She kept one hand on the wheel while she alternated massaging each sore side, hand expressing milk that spilled down her front. Milk that should have been in Celia's tummy. Téa trembled, craving to have her daughter safe in her arms. She raised her head to the sky above as tears fell down the side of her face, and a silent wail rose to the heavens.

The SUV rocked side to side as it roved deep into the forest. When they could go no further, Téa and Zephyr got out, grabbed their backpacks of supplies, and began their trek. The remainder of the journey would have to be done on foot.

Téa walked as fast as she could, careful to watch her step as they made their way into the depths of the overgrown forest. When at long last she could make out the edges of a great lake, she started to sprint towards it and the rundown cabin in the distance.

Zephyr put an arm out and held her back. She shot him an intense glare. "What are you doing? We're almost there." Her words came out as a hushed yell.

He stepped in front of her and dropped his arm. "You can't just go running in there. We need to be careful. Keep your eyes open."

Téa knew he was right, her desperation had momentarily taken over and now her ears were suddenly alert to every brush of a leaf, every crunch of a branch. They crept towards the falling apart log home with its front door wide open. When they didn't see or hear anyone else, Téa led Zephyr to the hidden entrance inside the cabin, that led into the old mining tunnels underground.

She felt for the string that ran along the dirt wall, the earthen dampness invading her nose. She whispered. "It's pitch black down here once we get away from the opening. Feel for the cord along the wall, don't let go of it, stay close."

Zephyr didn't say anything in response, but she felt his hand on her back. She took careful steps forward, listening for any other signs of life.

They had been walking for at least a half-hour when Téa heard a cry ahead of them. Her pace quickened with Zephyr on her tail. Her heart ached and her pulse raced.

A booming voice and a blinding light stopped her in her tracks.

"STOP RIGHT THERE!" The rough voice shouted out. "Take your packs off and slide them forward!"

They did as they were told and the scene in front of them came into focus. Téa's heart sank as she recognized the middle-aged man with black hair as Louis, who ran the grade school at the sanctuary with his wife Tess. She was shaken by surprise, but her mind cleared at the soft sound of a baby, *her* baby, crying somewhere nearby.

Focus.

"Louis? What is this? Did you steal Celia from me? Why?" Téa shook her head in disbelief and searched for the place where Celia's cries were coming from. It was difficult to see past the floodlight that shone in her eyes.

Louis raised a handgun and pointed it directly at Téa, snot and tears ran down his dirt-covered face. "Because, you have to bring her back, you have to bring Tess back."

Bile climbed her throat as Téa recalled the images of Tess running away from the General's men and being shot in the back, remembering as she fell and drowned in a pool of her own blood. Téa's voice came out shaky. "Louis, Tess is dead, you know this, I can't bring her back."

The man's eyes grew, a wildness about him scared Téa as he screamed at her. "LIAR! You brought Zephyr back; you can bring my Tess back too!"

How did he know about Zephyr being back so soon? Was someone surveying Sandstone?

She could feel Zephyr squeeze her wrist trying to lend her his emotional strength. Téa cleared her mind and focused on the metal weapon that Louis held. Using her mind, she yanked it from his hand.

"NO!" Louis shouted as he ran, dipped down, and picked up Celia where she had been crying in a basket on the floor. He spoke quickly. "You can bring Tess back first and then Celia too." The man sobbed as his hand dangerously curled around the baby's tiny frail body.

A lump formed in Téa's throat, her feet were heavy as lead, her voice desperate. "Please Louis, I don't have the power to bring people back from the dead. Please, don't hurt my baby."

Out of the darkness Elijah crept up behind Louis, with one crutch raised he jabbed the man as hard as he could in the back. When Louis fell to his knees, Zephyr sprinted forward and grabbed Celia just as she fell from the man's hold before she hit the ground.

Chapter Fourteen
Eleanor

Eleanor sat on the ground of her opened holding cell. Just beyond where the bars used to be lay Amber, passed out from her efforts of trying to save her grandfather. Eleanor crawled over to her and cradled her head and shoulders on her lap, smoothing her hair back and wiping the tears that had fallen from her eyes, while she tried not to look at Fred's still body in the cell next to her.

Other women, mostly young but some old, began to come out from the other cells along the long cave-like corridor. The bright pink glow came from a sun-like orb that hung from the ceiling of the tunnels, despite its creator, Amber, being unconscious. The women shielded their eyes as they cautiously emerged.

Eleanor reluctantly looked at the cell directly across from hers and saw Fred's unmoving form, a pool of darkened red hugged his abdomen and clumped together with soil. She could see in the dirt where Fred struggled against his attacker. Footprints and long drags in the earthen floor shaped like long grotesque worms fighting their way to an escape that would never come.

The assailant's body was frozen stiff with the fear he faced in his death, his sins forever frozen on his ashen skin.

Hot tears trailed down Eleanor's cheeks, her lips glued shut with emotion, and hands that didn't seem like her own shook as she tried to process what was happening around her. Voices that seemed to flow to her from far away as though she were underwater, started to clear.

"Ma'am? Excuse me ma'am, are you okay? Are you injured?"

Eleanor slowly raised her gaze to meet that of a young girl speaking to her. Eleanor cleared her throat, but no words would come. She tried again and was successful this time. "No, I'm not injured. I'm okay." Her mind cleared enough to remember why she was here to begin with. She looked at the girl and asked. "I'm looking for a friend, her name is Mabel. Have you met anyone by this name?"

The young girl's eyes widened in excitement. "Yes! I know Mabel. She shares her bread slice with me at lunchtime." The girl's voice dropped to a whisper. "They keep her in isolation most of the time."

The other captives had started to crowd around. Eleanor and Amber were blocking the hallway, which was also the way to their freedom. Eleanor gently laid Amber down to the side to clear the passageway and stood up. "I know you're all scared, and ready to go home to your loved ones, and I won't stop you. But this battle against the loyalists is not one I can win alone. I can promise that if you walk away now, they will come for you, again, and again, until they get what they want." She paused, took a deep breath, and continued. "Please don't go yet, help me fight them. Anyone who can. Anyone who may have abilities, knowledge of this tunnel system, fighting experience, anything that could help us overtake them."

It was quiet for several seconds and Eleanors' pulse quickened. These were mostly scared children, and what she asked of them was monumental, Eleanor knew that. She held her breath knowing she would most likely be alone in the fight against the Loyalists, and her search for Mabel.

Just when she thought hope may be lost, a small voice from the back perked up. "I can go invisible." Another older voice. "I can teleport small distances." The various voices continued, one after another, speaking up with their abilities, and how they could help. Accelerated healing of self and others, the ability to freeze anything with a touch, the mental capability of bending another's reality, and half a dozen more.

Minutes later when it was quiet again, Eleanor couldn't help but ask. "Why stay prisoners all this time? You all could have escaped, gone home. Why haven't you fought?"

The oldest of the group stepped up to face Eleanor. "A single power isn't strong enough. They've threatened our families, and those who don't have families, they've threatened other prisoners. Anytime someone has fought back, the loyalist would pick a person and torture them, then kill them in front of us. We haven't been able to talk with each other. They keep us quiet, and in the pitch black so that we can't coordinate with each other." The old woman clenched her fists and continued. "But now is our chance. Now is our opportunity to fight back. Together, we can overtake the Loyalists."

Just then Amber stirred. Eleanor held her breath, knowing what the girl was waking up to. Amber slowly sat, and by the glow of the pink orb she went to her grandfather's body. She curled up onto Fred's chest and cried softly.

Eleanor wasn't sure how long they had before another guard would come. She crawled over to the girl and said quietly. "I'm so sorry for your loss, Fred loved you so much and he became a dear friend to me." Eleanor paused and took a deep breath. "But Amber dear, we must make a plan to escape while we still can." Eleanor worried about pulling Amber away; but Amber's internal strength surprised Eleanor when the girl said. "You're right. Now is not the time for grieving or running away, that will come later, now was the time to fight back." Amber looked at Eleanor with fire in her eyes, and for the first time Eleanor felt like they could win this battle.

Eleanor was behind a girl who had the ability to see in the dark. The girl was in the lead as the group walked single file and hunched over through the darkened tunnels, each holding the hand of the person in front of them. Only the quiet sounds of their breathing and shuffling feet would alert the guards, but Eleanor hoped it would not come to that. She hoped they would be able to take the guards by surprise and protect the remaining girls from harm.

The lead girl stopped abruptly with a "Shush." and Eleanor squeezed her hand in understanding. Eleanor whispered to the person on her other side, who had the ability to make herself and others invisible but only for short bursts of time. "Now". Eleanor held her breath as the loud thumps of a guard's footsteps passed by them and let out her shaky air in relief when she realized the group was not detected by the guards with their night vision goggles.

The tunnels were dark, insulated, and distant from each other, which, combined with the fact that the guards rarely fed or checked on the prisoners, bought them some time. But the guards walked around freely with night vision goggles, so the group had to take extra precautions to not be found until they reached their destination, operation central. One of the others was able to astral project, she had the entire layout of the tunnel system memorized. They only had another four tunnels to go before they would be in the room that controlled power to the entire tunnel system. Their plan was to overtake the two to three guards that were usually in the control room, turn on all the lights—which would temporarily blind every loyalist wearing his night-vision goggles—then open all the remaining closed cells and fight their way out together.

The group was just about to continue on their path when suddenly another guard came out of a hidden entrance. A seemingly solid wall slid to the side revealing a large opening to another room. He spotted them instantly and reached for his walkie-talkie. Before he was able to, one of the girls sprang forward with hands raised and touched him, the guard instantly froze in place and slowly turned into a solid block of human ice.

The girl jumped up and down in silent celebration, happy with the successful use of her powers.

Eleanor crept around him and peered into the darkness, she whispered to the girl who could see in the dark. "Can you see anything? Are there any other guards? What's in there?"

The girl only whimpered. "Oh no. Oh no oh no oh no."

Eleanor could hear the young girl begin to cry. She turned away and whispered down the line of girls. "Amber, can you go in there and turn on your glow?"

"Yes." Amber replied.

The sounds of Amber's shuffling feet moved forward towards the opening of the hidden door. Her beautiful powerful pink glow illuminated the room, and Eleanor watched her drop to her knees.

Eleanor walked into the lit-up room and gasped in terror. It was the Connex-B boys. The loyalists had indeed continued their experiments and the results were horrendous.

Dozens of boys, some teenagers, some only toddlers, were suspended in a clear liquid inside tall, large cylinders.

Tubes coming out of all of them. Some were missing body parts; some were just parts in jars. Others were still being kept alive by machines; those were the worst to look at. A few were transformed entirely, barely recognizable as being human, skin stretched and muscle on the outside, monstrous looking.

"Oh my God. What have they done?" Eleanor whispered from behind her hand, failing to pull her eyes away from the horror in front of her. Heart breaking and nausea rolling in her stomach, able to continue, mostly from pure shock, when worn off, she would surely shatter. "I don't see any that can be helped, I don't think any would survive outside of whatever liquid they're being kept in. Come on, we need to go."

She turned to leave the room with Amber and the others, all of them ready to follow her, when she was stopped in her tracks by a raspy voice.

"*Kill me.*"

Eleanor stopped and looked to her left. A small boy was on a table reaching for her. It was clear he was being kept alive by unnatural and painfully cruel means.

He rasped again. "*Kill me, please.*"

Eleanor's heart ached and she shook her head as tears fell to the floor. "I can't."

One of the older women gently pushed past Eleanor and patted her on the shoulder as she went towards the boy on the table. The woman looked at a smaller silver table next to where the boy lay, sorting through various needles and glass bottles. She found what she was looking for and held it up. "Morphine." She pushed a needle into the bottle and filled the entire syringe. She gently smoothed the boys' forehead and whispered to him in a comforting way that only a mother can and pushed the needle into his skin. The boy relaxed and whispered, "Thank you." before closing his eyes and succumbing to his eternal rest.

The youngest of the group of girls sobbed into a puddle on the floor and one of the teenage girls bent to retrieve her, cradled her in her arms, and walked out of the room. Amber turned her glow off, and they continued on their way.

Outside the control room door, Eleanor whispered to a squat woman with disheveled rust colored hair and a sharp nose. "You're up." The woman slowly turned the handle and walked in. Seconds later they could hear men screaming. Three men came running out, waving their arms, and patting themselves as they ran, as though they were trying to put out an invisible fire on their bodies.

Eleanor smiled smugly at their distress and went inside to find that the room was well lit. She found a control panel and searched for the lighting system. She found the switch she was looking for, flipped it, and all the holes within the mountain came to life with bright light. Next, she found the switch for the cell doors and flipped it too.

Chaos ensued.

All throughout the tunnel system shouts echoed. The group of girls and women all ran off to their assigned tunnel to help the others who were now released. It didn't take long for this group of powerful women to overtake their loyalist captures once they were able to work together. And when all was quiet, Eleanor ran. Hallway after hallway, searching. Her heart raced, her legs were sore, her adrenaline and love was all that kept her going as she looked for her Mabel.

Finally.

She saw her. Her beautiful brown skin that always seemed to have a glow was now dry and peeling. Her face bloodied, and she was thinner than when Eleanor saw her last, but alive, and in one piece. Her chest blossomed with relief and heat rushed through her as she ran to Mabel and pulled her into an embrace.

Eleanor wiped the tears from Mabel's cheeks and kissed away her pain. Eleanor looked deep within her lovers eyes, and she couldn't imagine a greater joy as Mabel said. "You found me. I knew you would find me."

"Always." Eleanor replied.

Mabel squeezed Eleanor closer and spoke softly so only she could hear. "I love you, Eleanor."

Time seemed to slow as they smiled and held each other close. When at last Eleanor could bear to pull away, she said. "I love you too."

They kissed and Eleanor wiped away the blood from Mabels face as she pulled away. Eleanor took a deep breath and reluctantly said. "I need to call my niece. I saw a radio in the control room, come with me?"

"Everywhere you go, I go." Mabel gently squeezed her hand, and they headed back the way Eleanor had come.

Walking through the various tunnels Eleanor saw tearful and happy reunions everywhere. Friends, sisters, mothers, and daughters, all had been kept separate from one another for months. But intermingled in all the joy, was sorrow. There were the few who were looking for the person who would never arrive.

They were about to pass by a medical-looking room when Eleanor stopped. "Let's get your wounds cleaned up first, shall we?"

Mabel nodded, and for the first time Eleanor could see in Mabel what the toll of isolation had taken from her. Shadows hugged her dark eyes, her cheeks were sunken, and her hair was in a knotted mess.

The room was a disaster, papers scattered on the floor, equipment had fallen to the ground or had been tipped over. It was as though someone was trying to grab as much as possible before making an escape. Eleanor started to look through the various drawers and cabinets. She found some peroxide and a clean cloth, and a tube of antibacterial ointment. Eleanor began gently wiping away the grime from Mabel's face, which revealed numerous small cuts and bruises. Mabel whimpered from the pain and Eleanor's heart tightened for her.

After a few minutes Eleanor said. "There, good as new. You're so beautiful." Eleanor spoke softly to Mabel as she brushed back locks of her hair.

They were about to leave the room when an open computer screen caught her eye. Eleanor walked over to a large desk, and quickly glanced through an email that didn't appear to be sent yet.

The email was incomplete, and the computer monitor splattered red. Eleanor wiped away the blood from the screen and read.

The traitors have infiltrated. This may be my last entry. To summarize my findings. As of approximately six weeks ago today, all the rules have changed. We have noticed for some time now that our initial experimentations on Connex gene carriers have been drastically incomplete. We originally assumed that only a supraphysiologic surge of cortisol from extreme stress would trigger the necessary epigenetic modification.

We know now, that is not the only avenue, and it is no longer only males who carry the Connex-B gene, but females can as well. Connex-A genes are not nearly as rare as we once assumed. The extermination of Connex carriers simply made it appear that the population of special gene carriers was limited, this is false.

Six weeks ago, it was clear that something else triggered a majority of epigenetic changes, carriers no longer needed a catalyst for Connex gene activation, most could simply access their powers at will. I have my suspicions that the birth of the child from subject 85 triggered this massive change. Let us pray that our efforts at retrieving the child are successful.

There are no more rules gentlemen, I can no longer predict Connex gene outcomes, it is now only us against them. They must all be eliminated regardless of-

Eleanor looked around the corner of the desk and saw a dead middle-aged man in a lab coat covered in blood. She gasped in surprise.

Mabel jumped up with concern from where she sat across the room. "What is it?"

"Nothing, nothing you need to see, come on, let's get out of here."

As they continued their walk toward operation central, where the radios were, to try and reach Téa, they passed by Amber. She was seated on the floor hugging her knees to her chest with her back against the wall, and she smiled wide through her tears.

Eleanor bent down to look at her. "Amber? Honey, are you okay?"

Amber's eyes glistened with tears, but her grin spread ear to ear. "I can hear him, Eleanor, Poppa-Fred, he's still here, with me. I can see him as clear as if he were alive standing in front of me."

Eleanor knew better than to not believe Amber, after all the abilities she had seen today, seeing, and hearing the dead was not the most outrageous.

Eleanor laughed in relief at the chance to say goodbye to her friend. "Amber, sweetie, that's wonderful. Do you think... you could tell him..."

Amber's smile dropped and her expression became serious. "Eleanor, he says it's coming. We have to hurry. We're going to need all of them. All the supernaturals."

Eleanor wondered if maybe Amber had experienced too much trauma if maybe she was breaking. But Amber seemed coherent, and she continued. "I can only see Poppa because he was my soulmate. Soulmate matches stay with their partners until both have passed on. But Elijah- he can see them all. Téa hasn't let Annabelle in, her grief has blocked their connection. But Elijah knows it's coming. Oh my God, Eleanor, we have to hurry."

Concern etched into the lines of Eleanor's face as she scrunched up her nose and tried to remain calm. "Amber, honey, you're not making any sense."

Amber seemed to be seized in panic. She stood suddenly and raised her voice to a desperate plea. "Téa will understand, we need to radio her now. Hurry, we're almost out of time. It's coming."

Amber took off running down the hall, and Eleanor and Mabel hurried to catch up. They reached the control room and Amber rushed over to a PA system. She turned on the microphone and held it out for Eleanor. "First. You must stop all the supernaturals from leaving. Tell them we still need their help. NOW!"

Eleanor's body started to tremble. She wanted to think that Amber was losing her grip on reality. But her eyes were clear and the determination in her voice strong. Plus, how the hell did she know who Téa was? Eleanor hadn't mentioned her to Amber, the pair had just met.

She shakily took the microphone and tried to talk, nothing but a squeak came out. Mabel gently squeezed her shoulder and whispered. "You can do this, I'm right here with you."

Eleanor cleared her throat and tried again. "Friends. My name is Eleanor. With the help of countless others, I have freed you all today. I know you all have been through unimaginable trauma, and I do not wish to ask more of you, but I must. Please, if you have an ability, stay. I will not ask you to stay in this prison. We will all meet outside in half an hour. Please, help me."

Amber was alternating standing on each foot, and rubbing her hands together. "Well done Eleanor, well done."

Eleanor placed the microphone back down on the desk. "What exactly am I asking from them? Why do we need their help."

Amber hurriedly nodded her head up and down. "I'll explain, I'll explain it all. But we need to call Téa. She's at the Sanctuary, Fred told me. You know the channel, right? You need to call her now."

Amber rushed over to the radio and pulled a chair out for Eleanor to sit down in front of it. Hesitantly, and very confused, Eleanor took her seat. Switched the radio on and dialed in to the correct channel to reach the Sanctuary.

Chapter Fifteen
Zephyr

Téas' screams in the air around him quieted as if time had slowed down. Zephyr clung to his baby girl protecting her tiny head from hitting the dirt floor. The first time he had held her she was wrapped in a blanket, this time, their skin touched. Electricity crawled up his spine and down his arms as his daughter's small body touched his bare hand, and he knew then, felt it in every fiber of his being, his soulmate gene was activated.

He looked at Celia's gorgeous clear gray eyes that matched his own, and he could see his life again. Every memory that had been locked away came flooding back. Wave after wave of happiness, heartbreak, anger, and sadness crashed into him, frothing in his mind's eye threatening to drag him out to sea.

He was seven years old at Sandstone estate, at an adult celebration of some kind. Smiling at a little girl perhaps a couple years younger at the end of the grand dining room table. Her mother showed her what the Au Gus was for.

He was seven years old sitting in the back of his father's SUV, it was night. The General growled at him to stay put as he left the car. Zephyr looked out the back window at the crash, he saw two little girls, one looked familiar from the dinner party, someone was dragging her out as she screamed. His father got back in the car. "What was that daddy?"

The General's irritated response. "I've told you not to call me that! You address me as, Sir."

Eight years old and moving into a grand castle. "This is our home now Mama?"

His mother's eyes looked far away as she responded. "This is not our home, but yes we will live here now, remember our home is always you and me, together we make a home."

She perked up then and wiggled his chin in that loving way that only she knew how.

A teenager now, in the library, blood pooling from his mother's head, the General threatening him to never speak of it. Fear, heartbreak, and despair, a coldness that he did not know if it would ever fade seeped into him.

Warmth, happiness, hope, as he looked into her eyes for the first time, Téa. She was his person; he knew it with every fiber of his being from the first moment.

Celia, remembering holding his child for the first time, but this time with a full understanding of who he is and the love *she was made from. His baby, their little girl, her warm body, as she cooed and wiggled, and calmed in his arms.*

The new power coursing in his veins, and his understanding of it in an instant as easy as breathing, as though it were a piece of him all along but only now, he could access it, and use it he would, any means necessary to protect his family.

From under the waters of emotional turmoil, he could hear Téa's screams in the background, shrieking at him to hold on. Zephyr shook his head to clear the fog that was his life, to realize he had wandered away from the rope along the wall and they were both about to tumble into the depths of a miner's tunnel that dropped twenty feet. He renewed his gentle but firm hold on his crying daughter just in time to move away from the hole, and to see that Louis had sprung up and was charging towards him, shouting as saliva flew from his mouth.

Zephyr held onto Celia securely with one arm, raised his other palm with his fingers splayed, and pressed an invisible force shield out from his body, stopping Louis in his tracks. The man dropped to his knees and Zephyr placed a hand on the ground. He focused on the tree roots growing underground outside of the tunnel walls and pulled them forward with his mind. Cascading dirt sprayed them all as the roots shot out and wrapped themselves around Louis, immobilizing him.

Elijah stepped out on his crutches from behind the box-shaped flood light sitting on the ground. "Zephyr!" He shouted his relief and hurried towards Zephyr. "You found us! I knew you would come!"

Zephyr held Celia in one arm and wrapped the other around Elijah. "Of course, little man, I told you, it's you and me now. Although, I think we just added two to our party." Zephyr winked and tousled the boy's hair.

Elijah stepped back with a huff. "Well it took you long enough. I guess the girls can tag along, they ain't so bad."

Zephyr chuckled at Elijah. "And hey, you called me Zephyr, how'd you know that was my real name?"

"Well duh, Annabelle told me." Elijah responded. "She had to wait until you knew first."

As Zephyr tried to process that, Téa flew into his embrace crying tears of relief. She peeked into Celia's blanket, checking her face, fingers, and toes, before her words became muffled as she sobbed into his chest.

"Téa, I couldn't hear that." Zephyr laughed.

She pulled away and gently took her daughter, planting kisses all over their baby girl. "It's her, isn't it? Celia's your soulmate."

He rubbed his hand behind his neck and smiled. "How did you know?"

"The same thing happened to me, as soon as I touched Annabelle, my sister, I could feel my powers, access them, use them."

They took a long moment to look at each other, his heart raced, his face flushed. With the danger gone, and finally being reunited, all he wanted to do was touch her, hold her, and never let her go. He could feel heat coming from her body, she looked at him, her body language still unsure, she didn't know that his memories were back.

He took a step towards her, closing the small distance, placed a palm on her cheek and whispered. "I remember, Téa. I remember everything." He brushed her bottom lip with his thumb, moved closer, let out a breath and caressed her lips with his. She responded with more force and desire rose within him. He reached around her and pulled them close together as he moved his lips one last time and never wanted to let go of this kiss.

Elijah moaned. "Eww, grown-ups are gross. Can we leave now please? I'm hungry."

He could hear the eye roll in Elijah's voice. Zephyr laughed. "Yeah, kid, let's get out of here."

He stepped back but kept an arm around Téa as she held Celia, and they started walking further into the miner's tunnel following the string along the wall to guide them. The floodlight started to diminish as they walked away from it. As the darkness enveloped them once again, Zephyr let go of Téa in order to guide Elijah.

In the silence Zephyr finally found the courage to ask. "Elijah, did he hurt you? Did he hurt Celia?"

Elijah quieted, and Zephyr's pulse quickened, anxious to hear the answer.

Finally he said. "No, he didn't hurt us. He seemed sad about taking us, like he didn't want to. And he took really good care of Celia."

Zephyr sighed with relief. "That's good buddy. I'm sorry it took us so long to get you back."

Ever the sarcastic and happy boy, Elijah's voice was sharp in the dark. "Ha, you worry too much Zephyr, it was only one night."

He could feel the chuckle through Elijah's shirt as he helped to keep him on the right path.

Thank God for this kid.

After a few more minutes of quiet, Zephyr could hear Téa's uneasy voice from up ahead. "Elijah, little man, why didn't anyone at the Sanctuary stop him? Is there something happening at the Sanctuary?"

"What's the Sanctuary?" Elijah asked.

"I assumed that's where Louis was holding you and Celia, where did you guys sleep last night?"

"We slept in that old gross house at the beginning of the tunnels. It's probably older than even you Zephyr! And it stunk like old people."

Zephyr stopped and bellowed out his laughter.

Elijah's voice was irritated now. "What's so funny." He harrumphed.

"Nothing buddy, nothing."

Téa sounded a bit more relaxed. "The Sanctuary didn't know about the kidnapping. That's a good sign that they weren't in on it."

He remembered back to their time together at the Sanctuary, and how it turned out to not be all good as they had hoped it would be. His muscles tensed and he ground his teeth. His brother was there. The brother he didn't even know about before was alive. All of a sudden, he realized how much he had missed, how much he didn't know.

He tentatively asked. "What's my brother's name? What's he like?"

He could hear Téa's soft footsteps on the dirt floor pause before walking again. "He's wonderful, Zephyr, and he'll love you. I think you'll like him. He was a big help to me, after... I lost you. He was very supportive." She was quiet again before continuing. "And do you remember when I told you about the surgeons daughter? Emma? She's Ian's wife now. Ian, that's your brother's name."

She was quiet for a minute, and he started to feel uneasy before she spoke again. "I knew about him, before."

"What do you mean, Téa?"

"Florence told me about him before she brought me to the Vida Brigade. I was going to tell you, but she wouldn't let me go back to the Sanctuary that night, and then the revelation about Emma, and then, well, I'm sorry. I should have told you."

He could hear the sadness in her voice and all he wanted to do was wrap his arms around her. He longed to touch her, comfort her. "Téa, it's okay. Really, it's okay. There was a lot going on and we both thought we'd have more time." He cleared his throat and tried to smile through his voice in the darkness. "Speaking of time, I think I saw you. When my powers activated, I had some flashbacks of my life. I think they were showing me the path that led to Celia. It was you; you were my path. I saw you at Sandstone as a girl, and your parents' car wreck, and—"

His throat seized a lump formed in his throat and a single tear slid down his nose.

Téa's voice was soft and kind. "It's okay, Zephyr. It's okay. The same thing happened to me and Annabelle. Every forgotten memory, good and bad. I remember what it felt like, that wave of emotion pulling you down, I understand."

"I love you, Téa."

"Ditto."

His heart smiled at the memory and importance of that simple word between them.

"You're my Sea Star Téa."

"Ugh, grownups."

The musical joy of her laughter warmed him to his core. Light started to return as they neared the end of the tunnels. His heart hammered in his chest. He was finally going to meet his brother.

Chapter Sixteen

Téa

Cool pine-scented mountain fresh oxygen cleared out Téa's lungs. She would be happy if she never again had to drown in the damp hard mineral air of the darkened miners' tunnel.

Her jaw dropped as she took in the sight in front of her. The Sanctuary had grown. Gone were the hobbit hole-inspired homes she remembered. Now, it looked like they were standing before a fully functioning society who no longer lived in fear of being found by a corrupt Dunamis. Treehouses sat above them like a blanket of homes built in the sky. Brightly colored pathways scattered the ground which led to a multitude of cabins. When Téa took a closer look, she could see that the bright colors came from painted rocks. The painted pictures on the rock faces were gorgeous, adorable, and varied in skill. One with stick figures, another done by a child's shaky hand, and some so detailed they looked like a photograph. A rainbow of color and happiness snaked its way through the village. She smiled seeing that the Sanctuary seemed to be thriving.

It didn't take long for their small group to be noticed by a Sanctuary resident.

"Did you all just come through the miner's tunnel?" A younger boy about Elijah's age gaped at them as he spoke. "You know we don't have to use that way anymore. Supposed to use the front entrance now."

Téa smiled at the boy. "What's your name?"

The boy frowned. "I'm not supposed to talk to strangers."

He started to back away, but Téa gestured to the baby snuggled at her chest. "This is my daughter, Celia, and we're here to see her uncle, Ian. Do you know him or his wife Emma?"

"You mean Mr. Young? Yeah, I know him, he'll probably be at the hospital." The boy gave them a sideways glance as he took off running.

Téa looked at Zephyr. "Well, at least I know where that is. We won't have to start knocking on doors." She let out a small laugh of relief. "Come on, I remember the way, besides it'll be good to have the kids checked out anyway."

Zephyr wrapped an arm around her shoulders before planting a kiss on her head. "Sounds like a plan."

Elijah's crutches clacked against the rocks on the path, and Celia wiggled in her mother's arms as they walked. Téa crinkled her nose. "It smells like Celia needs a change too, and probably needs to eat."

Zephyr anxiously chuckled at her side. "You're going to have to show me how to do all the baby things. I'm guessing it's not as easy as it looks."

She gave him a reassuring caress down his arm. "Hey, I know it's a lot, but we'll figure it out together. I have a feeling you're going to be a natural." She winked.

It was a gorgeous day, a stark contrast to the events they had just endured, but graciously fitting to the outcome. They were whole again. Zephyr with a complete recollection of his life, Celia back in her arms, and she definitely had a soft spot for Elijah, but who wouldn't? The kid was remarkable. The beautiful blue sky shone through the leaves scattering the ground with heart-shaped light sprays. Background chattering of the Sanctuary residents floated around them with the occasional sharp cry of laughter.

They had walked only a few more feet when they crossed paths with Florence. The old woman still had her long silver hair and sparkling light blue eyes. Téa stopped in her tracks when she made eye contact with the old woman. The pair stared at each other. Finally, Florence cleared her throat and made a motion indicating that she was going to approach them. Téa ground her teeth and glared.

"Téa, it's wonderful to see you again, I'm so glad you finally brought the little one-"

Téa raised a hand. "Florence, stop. Just stop. I can't believe they let you walk around freely like this, if it was up to me, you'd be locked up for whatever years you have left."

Florence stood awkwardly, mouth ajar, making a small sound as though she was flabbergasted.

Téa dropped her arm from where she had held it signaling Florence to stop. "If you'll excuse us, I need to speak with Ian regarding the recent *kidnapping of my daughter.*"

Florence hesitated before moving out of the way. "Wait. Please. I can imagine what you must think of me, but I was only ever trying to do what was best for the Sanctuary. I was only ever trying to keep us all alive."

Téa angrily shook her head. "Now's not the time Florence-"

"Fine, but Ian isn't at the hospital, and you'll have to come and see me anyway if you need to discuss matters of security, I am still lead officer of the Vida Brigade."

Téa let out a shrill laugh. "You have got to be kidding me! You? You of all people are still in control?" She calmed her incredulous laughter and said with a steady voice. "Tell us where Ian is *now*, and then *please* get out of the way."

Florence sighed. "Look, it's obvious you all have been through something, whether you want to believe it or not, I only want to help. Go ahead and keep going to the hospital, get yourselves checked out, and I'll send Ian to you."

Téa was quiet but gave a small nod of acknowledgment and Florence stepped out of the way.

After a moment, Téa leaned towards Zephyr and angrily whispered. "I don't trust her Zephyr, and I never will." Her voice rose an octave. "How could Ian let this happen? After everything, I told him about her, and Emma is his wife now for cripes sake! I established the new Dunamis system. I should know who oversees military establishments! Right!?"

Zephyr raised Téa's hand to his lips and then covered it with his own as they walked. "I hear you; we'll figure it out together."

The hospital was one of the only structures that was not destroyed during the attack from the General's men and had remained largely unchanged. A giant semi-sphere, at least one hundred yards long, half above ground, and half below, completely made of stretched timber polished to a high shine.

Zephyr held the hospital door open for Téa and Elijah, and she noted the cool relief in temperature as they escaped the heat of the day. A kind familiar voice greeted them. "Téa! Is that you?"

"Jessop?" Téa smiled and held her arm out for an embrace from the brown skinned, middle-aged, balding man in glasses coming towards her. "It's wonderful to see you, Jessop!" She said.

Jessop clasped his hands behind his back and smiled. "And it is wonderful to see you. To what do we owe the honor of your presence."

Téa smiled. "Oh don't be so dramatic, I would have come eventually."

Jessop narrowed his gaze. "Meaning this visit wasn't planned?"

"Not exactly, it's a long story, the kids need to be checked out though, can you-"

"Woah, woah, woah, Zephyr?" Jessop stumbled back a step and clutched his chest. "We were told you died-" Shock spread across the man's face as he processed the fact that the person standing next to Téa was not Ian.

Instead of responding to Jessop, Téa turned to face Zephyr, realization in her eyes. "Florence knew you were alive, she wasn't surprised at all to see you, how could she have known you survived?"

Florence appeared in the doorway and cleared her throat. "Perhaps we can all discuss this privately in a room?"

Téa jumped a little at Florence's presence. Florence stepped around them and walked further down the hall revealing Ian behind her. He stood stock-still with his mouth slightly open. "Téa? Is this? So, it's true?"

Téa's pulse quickened, and she turned a little to take a quick glance at Florence, then looked back to Ian. Before anyone could say anything else, Celia started to cry. Téa had nursed Celia while they walked the miner's hall, grateful for all of her midnight feedings in the dark, and nursing while walking around Sandstone, it had given her the perfect practice to do what she needed to do one-handed while walking in the dark. Afterward, Celia had fallen asleep from the movement and a full tummy.

Now her baby girl was wailing to the heavens. The twins, Zephyr and Ian, had yet to say anything to each other, and Téa cleared her throat. "Ian, there's a lot we need to talk about." She paused and glared at Florence. The old woman should have told Ian more about his brother, like the fact that they were twins. "But we haven't seen our children in twenty-four hours. We need a few moments to check the kids out and take care of their needs first. I didn't think you would get here so quickly."

Ian only nodded; mouth still slightly ajar. Téa softly nudged Zephyr in his side. He was standing in stunned silence and still, neither twin said anything. Téa gently tugged on Zephyr's shirt bringing his attention back to her and Jessop, who was leading them to an examination room. Finally, Zephyr moved. Celia cried more furiously, and Téa calmly made shushing sounds and lightly bounced her as they walked.

She didn't want to ignore or downplay the brothers meeting each other for the first time, but they clearly needed some breathing room to process, and the children needed their attention.

When Jessop closed the door, he asked Téa. "Can you give me a brief summary about what's going on? Or rather the parts that affect the children and anything medically pertinent that I should know."

Téa answered Jessop as she carefully laid Celia down on the medical bed and removed her backpack. She proceeded to change Celia's diaper as she spoke to Jessop. "The children were kidnapped. This is Elijah, he's eight-".

"Eight and a half actually." Elijah said proudly, then scrunched his nose. "Ugh, that baby stinks." he said disgusted.

Téa laughed as she kept cleaning Celia. "Yeah a little bit. Anyway, Elijah said their kidnapper didn't hurt them, and all things considered, took good care of them." Téa finished changing Celia and sat on the medical table holding her.

Jessop took a deep breath. "I see. Okay, well let's start with some vitals, may I?"

Téa nodded. "Yes." Her emotions fluctuated all over the place, and the fear of something being wrong with her daughter consumed her, she shuddered as she held back a new wave of tears.

Zephyr noticed the change in Téa's body language. He sat next to her on the bed that was more like a soft table and rubbed her back in slow circles. He ran a single finger down Celia's soft cheek and smiled. "You're so strong, aren't you? Just like your Mama."

They looked at each other with love in their eyes and Celia cooed in happiness. Téa laid her head on Zephyr's shoulder as Jessop took Celia's heart rate and blood oxygen level with a monitor that wrapped around her tiny foot. He then gently looked over her general well-being, shining a light in her eyes and ears, moving her legs and arms to gently check her movement, listening to her heart, and breathing with a stethoscope. All while Elijah looked over from where he sat, Zephyr held onto Téa, and she held onto Celia. A family.

When Jessop was done, he stood up straight from being hunched over and smiled. "She's perfect, I see no signs of trauma."

Téa let out a deep breath of relief and smiled. "Thank you, Jessop."

"No thanks needed; it was my pleasure. Now, what about you sir?" He winked and looked at Elijah. "Mind if I give you a once over?"

Elijah shifted in his seat, obviously uncomfortable. "Um, can it just be Zephyr and me?" He said it quietly and averted his gaze.

Téa stood up and handed Celia to Zephyr as she put her backpack on. Then Zephyr handed Celia back, and Téa crossed the room to look at Elijah. "Hey buddy, it's okay, wanting privacy is perfectly reasonable, I'll see you both soon, okay?"

He nodded, and Téa turned to face Zephyr before leaving. "I'm going to find an empty room, and nurse Celia, come find me when you're done?"

He stood and gave her a quick peck on the cheek. "Yes, I'll find you anywhere." He smiled and wrapped an arm around her waist in a loose embrace. "Hey, I love you." He said and her heart skipped a beat and warmth crept up her sides. "I love you too." She grinned from ear to ear as she closed the door behind her.

About thirty minutes later Téa had finished feeding Celia and there was a knock at the door to the empty room she had found. "Who is it?"

"Jessop."

"Come on in."

Jessop poked his head in. "Zephyr is waiting for you down the hall in room three. I offered to watch the kids for you while you meet with Florence and Ian, if you'd be comfortable with that?"

Téa was hesitant, her mama bear instincts screaming at her to never put Celia down ever again, but she had to start somewhere, and she trusted Jessop. "Yes, thank you, it's probably best if they aren't in the room."

She couldn't place a reason for the nerves that were needling at her as she walked down the hall, poking her in all of her insecure spots, anxiety riding her shoulders like a second person taking a piggyback ride.

Room number three was a long conference room with big clear windows that looked out to the rest of the hospital. It had one long table and half a dozen swivel chairs. Florence, Ian, and Zephyr were already inside. The tension in the room was thick as Téa eased inside. It was quiet, and nobody smiled. Everyone stood with their arms crossed in separate corners of the room.

Téa cleared her throat. "Hi. Ian, long time no see!" She waved weakly and said sarcastically having seen him only days ago.

Ian didn't acknowledge her humor. "Why didn't you tell me my brother was alive, Téa?" He leaned in a corner with one foot crossed over the other, he stood up straight now. "Why didn't you call me?"

Florence interrupted then. "Yes, Téa, you should have informed us of the situation considering your meeting point was just outside of our borders. I could have sent a search party out."

Téa scoffed. "Forgive me for not thinking clearly when my child was taken, we had to act quickly." She glared at Florence. "Also, why exactly would I trust you? Do you really think I'd put my child's safety in your hands?"

Florence was about to respond when Ian jumped in. "What about me? Do you not trust me anymore? Celia is my niece, Téa, you should have told me."

Zephyr was the one to interrupt next. "Look obviously we are all getting off on the wrong foot, let's just take a step back-"

Ian raised his voice. "No. Téa should have known better." He turned towards Téa standing only a foot away and pointed a finger. "You should have involved the Sanctuary; it was a stupid and dangerous move to try and handle this on your own."

Zephyr crossed the room in two swift steps, placing himself between the two. His voice was like ice, cold, smooth, and strong. "Do not speak to my family that way. Don't you ever talk to her like that again."

Ian got in Zephyr's face, anger radiated off him. "She is more family to me than you could ever be! Brother or not, I don't know you. I don't trust *anything* that could come back from the dead. For all we know, you had this planned all along, with your father, the General."

Téa knew at that moment that Ian had gone too far. There was nothing she could have done to stop the punch that Zephyr hurled at Ian. The hit connected with Ian's jaw with a hard *whack.*

She reached deep within herself to pull forward the Connex-A powers that had been dulled ever since Annabelle's death. Those powers that were so interconnected to her soulmate, she had buried them deep trying to escape the pain of her sister's loss. But now, seeing the brother's fight broke her heart, she was desperate to open that emotionally closed box and reach for every tool in her arsenal.

Hunched over from the effort of trying to access her dormant abilities, Téa pounded her fists on the ground once and shouted. "Enough!" Ian and Zephyr were flung apart, each landed on their backside at opposite ends of the room.

Ian coughed and grabbed his chest where the invisible force had made the most contact. "Fuck, Téa, what the hell?"

Florence took a step, and Téa raised an arm in her direction. "*Don't fucking move.*"

Florence halted, and Zephyr groaned. Téa hurried over to him and put a hand behind his head to check for any injuries. "I'm so sorry, I didn't mean for that to come out so hard. I was just trying to push you away from each other." Zephyr sat up, and Téa helped him. "Are you okay?"

He nodded. "Yeah, I think I'm fine." He raised his eyes to hers. "I'm sorry too." He looked at Ian. "I shouldn't have hit you." He added begrudgingly.

Florence cleared her throat. "Perhaps we can all start over-"

Téa stood. "I don't want to hear another thing from you. You knew Zephyr was alive, I know it. What else are you hiding, Florence?"

Ian's voice was firm. "Téa, now is not the time for your accusations against Florence, I trust her, and you need to trust me. We need to focus on the kidnapping and what it might mean for the Sanctuary."

Téa gaped at Ian, her voice shrill. "Are you kidding me right now, Ian? She needs to be questioned. We didn't get any information out of Louis. Which, by the way, we left him tied up in the miner's tunnel, he's about mid-way if you want to send someone to retrieve him."

Florence stared wide-eyed at Téa. "Why on earth didn't you say something sooner!? That poor man."

Téa laughed a sick and angry chuckle. "Are you *serious* right now? That *poor* man *kidnapped* our children. You and he should both be locked up!"

Florence huffed and hurried out of the room, shouting over her shoulder. "I'm going to go get Louis, you all work this out on your own."

Téa gestured towards Florence walking out and looked at Ian. "Really, you're just going to let her leave?"

Ian took a deep breath and sat at the table. "Téa, you have to let go of whatever ill will you're harboring against Florence, Emma has forgiven her, and you should too."

"Ian, this isn't about forgiveness, this is about her being guilty. She knows something, I feel it."

Ian rubbed his temples. "You don't think maybe you're letting your personal feelings towards her influence you? It's a little hypocritical don't you think? Jessop probably knew what Dr. Anderson was doing to his daughter. This is a small hospital that only had three doctors at the time, Jessop had to have known, why be so forgiving towards him? Hell, half the Sanctuary probably knew, why are you taking all your anger out on Florence?"

Téa sighed and dropped her head. "It's not just that she allowed Emma to be abused by her father. It's that she helped him to do it. She supplied the drugs." She sat down across the table from Ian. "Not only that, but she also wasn't surprised to see Zephyr at all, she knows something, Ian. And if she's head of the Vida Brigade, why didn't she know what Louis was up to? She's hiding something, why can't you see that." Téa took a deep breath and continued, "Florence was going to blow up every bit of Dunamis food, killing thousands of people, she was going to blow up the space station, or take control of it for herself. We never did find out what her plans were for that. I've told you all of this before."

Téa stopped talking, and her lip quivered. Ian reached across the table with palms up, Téa put her hands in his, a tear rolled down her cheek. "She betrayed me, Ian. She used me. Whose side are you on?"

"Yours of course, always yours. But Téa, you need to trust me on this. Florence... well, you need to sit down and have a conversation with her. For now, please just trust me. She is not our enemy."

Ian stood and looked at Zephyr. "Would you both like to take a break? I think the danger has passed for the time being. Why don't you come to our house and get something to eat, and let the kids rest?"

Zephyr nodded, and Téa rose from her chair. "That sounds nice. I could use a good Emma hug right about now anyway."

She reached her hand out for Zephyr to take, he intertwined their fingers and kissed her on the head. They collected Celia and Elijah, and Ian led the way home.

Chapter Seventeen
Zephyr

Anger, confusion, sorrow, disappointment, and hurt, all turned to liquid and swirled around inside of Zephyr, a Molotov cocktail ready for throwing at any enemy target. He got his memories back and in the process, stepped into a life he did not recognize. The only familiar constant being his love for Téa, he held onto her like his own personal rescue boat in a storm.

Then there was this overpowering new feeling from his soulmate gene being activated with his daughter Celia. This was not a passionate connection, but something more. Something like what he experienced during patrols when his platoon had his six. As long as she was near, he had a sense of power and protection, with his new abilities, which mixed with the intense and overwhelming love that a father has for his daughter. She was an extension of him, he sensed every shift in her emotions. It was almost as if he could see the world through her eyes and losing her would be like losing a piece of himself.

His two lives clashed together in his mind. Trying to sort out each piece of a puzzle into its own spot had given him a headache. When Téa first told him he had a brother, he couldn't wait to meet this person, his one sliver of hope for having a family. Then his memories flooded back, and he realized he already had a family, and he didn't know where a long-lost brother would fit in, and not just any brother, but an identical twin that the General had hidden from him.

Who was this person, this brother that he was supposed to accept without question? Would he be a threat, was he hiding something? Nothing that the General had anything to do with could possibly be good. He himself had only survived to become a decent person because of the love from his mother until her death. Who did his brother have to keep him on the straight and narrow?

And now they were headed into the lion's den. Ian's home. Every one of his molecules was on edge, rushing around a glass beaker fighting to get out. He looked at Elijah, Celia, and then Téa as they walked and that brought him some calm. He tried not to make eye contact with Ian. He should not have punched him, but Ian deserved it, he was being an ass.

Zephyr must have been visibly twitching with anxiety because Téa reached for his hand and said. "Are you okay?"

He forced a smile, the last thing he needed was her worrying about him. "Yeah, I'm good, just looking forward to resting for a minute, it's been a long couple of days."

She laughed, God that laugh, he could listen to it for an eternity and never tire of her sound. "You could say that again. I'm praying for at least a four-hour stretch from Celia. It would be nice to get caught up on some sleep."

He rubbed his thumb along hers as they held hands. "We can take turns checking on her when she wakes up, we're a team remember, always and forever."

She blessed him with another one of her glorious smiles and his heart skipped a beat. She looked up at him. "I've missed you Zephyr, more than you could possibly ever realize."

He didn't know what to say to that, it made him feel guilty, but his absence was not his fault. So instead, he raised her hands to his lips and gently placed a kiss before throwing her a smile. "So, Emma, that's *the* Emma, right? The surgeon's daughter?"

Ian cleared his throat. "Please don't talk about my wife."

"Aye, aye, captain." Zephyr replied sarcastically as he lazily saluted.

Ian stopped and Zephyr almost ran right into him. "Is this all some kind of big joke to you?"

Zephyr rolled his shoulders. "No, *brother*, I don't find any of this *funny*."

"Good." Ian turned around and kept walking.

Téa gave Zephyr a sideways glance. "Are you sure you're okay?"

He wasn't sure if he was or not and needed a change of topic, he stared into her eyes for a moment, before clearing his throat and forcing a smile. "So, it seems like you kind of took over for the General, for a while at least. What's that been like?"

She narrowed her eyes at him, obviously aware of his change in conversation, but thankfully she didn't push the issue and instead responded. "It's kept me busy. In the beginning, Ian and I first set up rescue missions to retrieve all the Connex-B boys that were being experimented on. They didn't have anywhere to go, and nothing to do, so most of them volunteered to help us bring seeds and supplies to the different towns and villages. Honestly, I think it helped them more than us. I saw a lot of emotional healing through their work."

Zephyr nodded his head to show her that he was still listening, and she continued. "After that, we had to focus on getting telecommunications back up and running. The foundation was still there to bring back landline telephones. It just needed repairs. Producing the actual telephones has been more difficult, which is why it's still so sparsely available in most areas. When I found out I was pregnant with Celia, I decided to take a back seat in the process of rehabilitating the nation. The heads of Dunamis still keep me mostly informed about what's going on, but I think it's more of a courtesy. I was never an actual official. I only had a kind of authority because I killed the General and because my abilities were so powerful."

Zephyr paused, then leaned forward to peer in her eyes before he continued to walk. "Wait a minute—*you killed the General?*"

She looked on edge, but he laughed. "That's my girl! I heard rumors, I don't know why I didn't connect the dots earlier."

When she didn't smile back, he realized that probably wasn't the best response. "I mean, that must have been horrible. Do you want to tell me about it?"

He saw her stiffen. "No. Maybe another time."

He was feeling uncomfortable again when Elijah chimed in laughing. "Sure are a ladies' man, aren't you Zephyr?"

"Shush kid, where'd you learn a phrase like that anyway? You're only eight." He glanced quickly at Elijah with a small smile.

Elijah puffed his chest out. "Eight in a half actually, and I heard my mom say it to my dad once."

Zephyr shook his head and chuckled softly, then looked back to Téa with sincerity. "I'm sorry Téa, that was insensitive of me, it's never easy taking a life, even if that life is the General. I really would like to hear about what you had to go through while I was gone, when, or if, you're ready."

She only gave him a small smile and somehow that only made the pit in his stomach grow. He was sinking again.

Finally, after what was likely only minutes, but felt like an hour, they arrived at Ian's home. Ian opened the door and gestured them all inside. "Welcome, come on in."

He was greeted by a savory scent wafting throughout the house as they opened the front door, and Ian yelled out to Emma announcing their arrival. Zephyr helped Téa with her backpack as she shrugged it off to the ground, then he removed his own.

The entrance led into a large front room that opened into the kitchen where they could see Emma cooking something at the stove and a little girl, who must be Nora, in her playpen. Elijah swiftly made his way to one of the couches in the front room, set his crutches to the side, and let out a long and dramatic sigh as he plopped himself into the cushions.

Zephyr chuckled at Elijah, then took Celia when Téa handed her to him so that she could rush off into, what he could only assume, was a much-needed embrace from Emma. His thoughts warmed as he watched his love get much needed comfort from her friend.

Celia cooed in his arms, his daughter relaxed in his embrace, and he could feel the joy coming from her. She loved being held by him and he loved holding her. He took in every little tuft of curly hair, every twinkle in her eye, the way her chubby tiny hand curled around his finger. She was perfect. How could he have possibly been responsible for creating something so amazing as this little human?

Téa came back and held her arms out for their daughter and Zephyr tried to hand her back, but Celia cried out and clutched onto Zephyr's shirt. Téa's face dropped again, and she let her arms down. "I guess she needs a little more daddy time."

Zephyr saw the effort Téa made to smile and the guilt gnawing at him amplified, he hated hurting her, even unintentionally.

It seemed as if Ian did one good thing. He must have explained everything to his wife, as Emma didn't ask any questions or seem surprised at the fact that Zephyr was alive, and that he was some kind of surrogate to a young boy. At least they didn't have to go through the unpleasantness of trying to talk through everything again.

Emma called out from the kitchen that dinner was ready, and Elijah shouted. "Finally, I'm starving!"

Zephyr chuckled at his dramatic sigh, and they all gathered around a dining table in between the kitchen and living room.

Zephyr balanced Celia in one arm and picked up his fork with the other. "What is this Emma, it looks amazing."

Emma smiled. "It's penne pasta with homemade vodka sauce and fresh herbs, all grown here in the Sanctuary." She said proudly. "Actually, Florence taught me the recipe."

He heard Téa choke on her food and made to move to her side, but relaxed when she took a drink of her water.

Her voice had lost all its laughter when she said. "Can we please not talk about Florence right now. How on Earth you could ever forgive her, let alone trust her is beyond me."

Zephyr watched Ian shoot Téa a tense glare. "Take it easy Téa. Like I said, you need to sit down with her."

Zephyr could sense the tension rising and interrupted just as Téa was going to respond. He swallowed his bite and looked at Emma. "I'm sorry, I didn't even formally introduce myself–"

Emma held up a hand and waved him off. "No, not needed, I obviously know who you are, I'm just happy you're here, for Téa." She grinned and looked at her friend.

He saw Téa's cheeks turn a shade of red out of the corner of his eye, and said. "Well, thank you for this delicious meal, and for having us."

Ian grumbled and Zephyr was sure Emma kicked him under the table before she said. "It's our pleasure."

There wasn't much conversation held after that. They practically inhaled their food after not having a decent meal in over twenty-four hours.

Afterwards, Emma told them that Nora would sleep with Ian and herself that night so that Elijah could have her room; and that they had set up an air mattress in the nursery where Téa and Zephyr could sleep with Celia.

Téa thanked Emma and Ian, and excused herself, Zephyr, and Elijah from the table. They were walking down the hall to the bedroom when Zephyr whispered. "Is it just me, or is no one besides you happy that I'm back from the dead?"

Téa stopped in her tracks and whispered back in a serious tone. "You have to stop saying that, Zephyr. You were never dead, you're not a zombie, you didn't rise from the grave. *Apparently*, there are actually people out there who believe that, and can you blame them? You were the General's right-hand man for many years. They don't know you the way I do."

The reminder of being his father's puppet punched him in the gut. "I wasn't his fucking right-hand man Téa, I was basically his prisoner, just like everyone else!"

Téa didn't raise her voice, and he could see the hurt in her eyes. He instantly regretted losing his temper when she said. "Don't speak to me that way, Zephyr. I know that. They don't." She took a deep breath before continuing. "I think maybe you should sleep in Elijah's room tonight. Celia and I will take the nursery."

He nodded in agreement and started to hand Celia over to Téa, but again Celia whimpered and clutched his chest. He could see Téa's eyes start to well with tears, and it crushed him to say. "Téa, I'm so sorry, but I think she wants to stay with me right now. I can feel her emotions, why don't we all stay together in one room?"

His heart ached as he watched the light seep out of Téa, her beautiful smile dulled to a thin line. She dropped her gaze. "No, it's okay, you and Elijah take the nursery with Celia, I'll take Nora's room."

His stomach clenched as he watched her walk away. It hit him then, and he chastised himself for not realizing it sooner. She told him back at Sandstone while he was still Theo, that she had a sister, Annabelle. Then in the tunnels, she mentioned her soulmate connection with Annabelle, *the* Annabelle that Elijah had been hearing through the radio.

How could I be so stupid, so blind?

Téa was grieving for more than just him, and she wasn't ready to talk about it. What else had he missed? Why didn't she want to talk to him?

He was tempted to run after her but thought it best to give her some space tonight. Tomorrow, he would put his emotional struggles aside and focus on Téa, the love of his life. He would bring her back to him.

Chapter Eighteen
Téa

Téa paced in Nora's room, somehow the distance between her and Zephyr felt greater than she could ever recall. She was not jealous of Zephyr's soulmate connection with Celia, the opposite in fact, she was overjoyed that her daughter would have such a meaningful relationship with her father. But it was hard to suddenly not be the center of her daughters universe, and she also found herself missing Annabelle more and more. Oh, how she craved just one last hug from her sister. How could she possibly ever tell Zephyr everything she had gone through while she thought he was dead, everything that she had done? She could still feel the ash in her lungs from all those soldiers, the lives that she cremated at will.

Despite the exhaustion overtaking her body, she could not get her mind to be quiet, she tossed and turned as sleep evaded her. Zephyr was changing in front of her eyes. She was losing him, and she didn't know why. If only he would confide in her, tell her what he was thinking. But wasn't she guilty of holding back as well? How could they meet each other in the middle and get back to the place they once were. She tried to push her thoughts aside, laid down, and closed her eyes.

Twice throughout the night, she heard Celia cry out from down the hall. She was astonished at how in tune a mother could be to the specific frequency of their children. She sleepily stumbled her way to her daughter and tried not to resent Zephyr for sleeping soundly through her cries. Téa changed and fed Celia each time, quiet as she could be, to not wake Elijah.

Téa was already up when the very first soft rays of light seeped in through the window. She needed to work out some of this tension and she knew exactly what to do. She was going to have that sit down with Florence that Ian kept insisting on. She could take her frustrations out on the old hag and expose her for the traitor Téa knew her to be. Celia would not be due for another nursing session for at least two hours, so Téa quietly got herself dressed and snuck out of the Young family home.

It was a cool morning and Téa wished she had a sweater with her. She wrapped her arms around herself as she listened to the musical chirps of the birds greeting the day. The grass underfoot was soft and spongy from the early dew. A spider's web caught rays of light which refracted around like a crystal in the sun.

The Sanctuary had grown so much, it took her longer than she anticipated to find Florence's house. But find it she did, and it was exactly as she remembered. Téa was irritated by the nostalgia she felt at seeing Florence's house, her once upon a time safe haven.

She rapped on the door incessantly until Florence flung it open. "What!" The old woman straightened her night robe. "Oh, it's you, well come on in then."

Florence shuffled out of the way and Téa stormed in with arms crossed and jaw set. "I know you're a traitor, you had something to do with Celia's kidnapping, I know it! You weren't surprised at all to see Zephyr; how could you have known he was still alive unless you were in cahoots with the Loyalists!?"

Florence worked her way into the kitchen, calm as a nun in church. "Well, good morning to you too. Would you like some coffee dear? And 'cahoots' really?"

Téa's jaw dropped. "Are you kidding me right now Florence? That's all you have to say."

The old woman sighed, filled two cups with coffee, placed one in front of Téa, and took a seat at the table. "If you're quite finished, we have a lot to discuss."

Téa hesitated; this was not at all the reaction she had expected. She reluctantly sat down.

"Now, that's better." Florence smiled. "Where shall I begin?"

"How about you start by telling me when you decided to betray the Sanctuary, to betray *me*?" Téa hated that her voice broke at the end of that sentence.

Florence reached for Téa's hand, but Téa pulled away and shook her head.

"Téa, dear, I'm not a traitor, and I never betrayed you. I simply was not surprised to see Zephyr because I knew for some time now that he would be coming back to you, that he was alive."

Téa ground her teeth to keep her chin from quivering. "How? And why? Why wouldn't you tell me that he was alive?"

Florence took a deep breath. "Because it wasn't time yet."

Téa tried to pull on her strength to put some authority back into her voice before she spoke. "What do you mean by that? Florence, stop talking in riddles and just tell me what's going on."

Florence picked at an old stain on her small round table. "You know, I was one of the first to receive abilities." She took a deep drink from her steaming mug, gulped, and sighed. "For the longest time, I didn't understand what was happening to me. It was just after the old world began to fall, and I didn't have anyone to turn to. My husband died from starvation early on." A hitch in Florence's voice threatened to dissolve Téa's resolve, but the old woman continued. "He insisted that I take his rations, he refused to eat to ensure that I had enough. You see, our daughter was pregnant at the time, with the twins, and my husband knew that our daughter would need me."

Téa was struggling now to see Florence as a bad person, but she remained upright and stiff in her chair as Florence continued her story.

"You see, the General's researchers got so much wrong about the Connex genes and their abilities. It started small, just flashes at first, and I didn't know what to make of them. I thought it was from lack of nutrition, hallucinations. We were out of food, my daughter, her husband, and myself, were desperate. We decided to raid the General's food storage."

Florence took a small gasp of air. "Well, you know how that ended." She wiped a tear from her eye. "After that, I had my first full vision. It wasn't just a flash, but more like a full-length feature film that played out in front of me. I thought I had lost my mind, but then my vision came true, I had seen the future."

Téa's eyes went wide, she believed Florence, but her resentment had solidified so much that she said. "*Liar.*"

Florence unsuccessfully reached for Téa's hand a second time. "I know you believe me dear; you're going to have to let go of your anger towards me."

Téa was incredulous. "How could I possibly believe that. Everything that has happened... if you could see the future, why would you let it all happen?" Téa's legs trembled, her heart pounded in her chest, her vision zeroed in on Florence. The old woman's silver hair suddenly seemed to be illuminated like a halo surrounding her mass of wrinkles. "You knew? This whole time, you knew and didn't stop any of the pain, any of the heartbreak."

Florence took a deep breath and reached for Téa's hands a third time, but Téa pulled back. Florence sighed. "It was the only way."

"Bullshit! There had to be another way. Zephyr didn't need to die, Emma didn't need to be..." Téa choked on her words before clearing her throat and continuing. "She didn't deserve what her father did to her, and you just let it happen." Her words trailed off at the end and she glared at Florence as she sniffled.

Florence's voice was desperate. "Téa... if there were any other way, I would have found it. I went through scenario after scenario in my head. Over and over and over again. I tried every possibility in my mind's eye, and we failed every time."

Téa glared at Florence. "You didn't try hard enough!"

Florence's voice was no longer calm and soothing, but she refrained from yelling. "You don't understand, I'm not invincible, I can't just sit down and play out a million scenarios in my head within seconds. For me, every time I tried seeing a new reality, it was like I was living it. Those ten different scenarios I tried, they were not just ten minutes, for me, it was ten years."

Téa narrowed her eyes at the old woman. "What do you mean by that? You mean it felt like you lived ten years?"

Florence sighed. "No. Each minute literally takes one year of my life away. If I try to see the future for too long, I'll age to my death."

This shocked Téa to silence for only a moment but she pushed her sympathy aside and stood fast and stared Florence down. "Why were you trying to live out different futures to begin with?"

Florence gulped. "The world is ending."

Téa cackled with disbelief. "Newsflash! The world already ended, and we're rebuilding, no thanks to you."

Florence rubbed her slippered toe against her hardwood floors. "No Téa, not The Decline. The entire Earth will be demolished, three days from now our planet will cease to exist. The things that have happened needed to transpire the way that they did, in order for us to save humanity."

Téa's whole body shuddered with fear and pent-up emotion, she clutched her arms around her chest. "Prove it, tell me why we had to endure all this pain in order to save ourselves. How will our pain save the world."

"Téa, you must understand, I did not get this ability until after my husband died. The Decline had already begun, surgeons among other people with necessary skills were not as abundant." Florence shook her head and continued. "In my mind, in the different version of our future, I found three other surgeons, all of them failed in saving Zephyr's life after the accident."

Téa could no longer hold back her tears. "He wouldn't have wanted Emma to go through that for him, he wouldn't have wanted to be saved at that point."

Florence stomped her foot. "You don't understand, it wasn't just about him! He needed to meet Elijah. Zephyr had to survive."

Téa shouted now. "Then why not lock the surgeon up until it was time to save Zephyr, why continue to supply him with the drugs?"

Tears streamed down Florence's face. "I tried that version of the future too, that man wasn't built to be locked up. He found a way to end his life every time." Florence gulped. "And when I didn't supply the drugs, he'd get them himself. He ended up getting greedy every time, overdosing Emma again and again, he'd lose his self-control, his sense of reason." Florence's words came out quickly now, talking animatedly with her hands. "I tried taking her away, and he would move on to hurting other women in his care. I tried *everything* Téa for a better alternative. I did the best I could, maintaining as best I could. Keeping her at my house as often as I could. Limiting his supply of Rohypnol."

Téa dug her toe into the floor and refused to look at the old woman. "Why not have Hue rescue us from Sandstone before the plane crash? There had to have been a way."

Florence was shouting now. "Stop it! Téa, can't you see how this has traumatized me? Broken my heart over and over again! Just stop. I tried a rescue, multiple times. Sandstone was a fortress, all of the Vida Brigade died trying to rescue you. We tried intercepting you once you got out, you believed us to be the general's men before we could ever get close enough. Téa, I tried everything. This was the only way. The way the universe wanted it. It was out of my control to change."

Téa collapsed internally and let her tears fall. She sucked in breath after breath, while the sobs racked her body. After some time, when the pain finally eased enough to talk, she asked, "What else aren't you telling me? What happens now? How exactly does the world end and humanity continue on?"

Florence slowly sat down next to her. "It doesn't matter how; it just matters that we win. We survive, and our children and grandchildren have a chance at life."

Téa wiped her tears and was quiet for a long time before she looked at Florence. "So, you were never going to blow up the space station, or Dunamis food supply, were you?"

Florence shook her head. "No, I knew it would never come to that. I just needed you to have a strong enough reason to go back to the General. If it was just you finding out about Emma, you would have confronted me. You didn't have powers yet, and you hadn't seen powers yet, so you would not have believed me. You would have had me silenced, locked up, and you would have lived a happy life with Zephyr until the planet was destroyed. The end."

Téa was quiet for a long moment again before asking. "How Florence? How does the world end? Tell me."

The old woman seemed to have aged even more since the last time Téa saw her, more wrinkles, her streaks of dark were gone and replaced with all gray hair. But the brightness in her eyes was still there, shimmering as she looked out upon the world. Florence took a deep breath and said. "It's the moon. The asteroid that hit Zephyr's farm, it was just a small bit of debris from a much larger meteor. *That* meteor is headed straight for our moon. It will break and rain down on Earth."

A sharp intake of breath, mind scrambling and heart racing. "Oh my god. How do we survive that? What are we going to do?"

Téa finally allowed Florence to take her hands into her own, and the old woman pulled her close. "We wouldn't survive that. We're going to evacuate earth before it hits."

Chapter Nineteen
Téa

eath itself stood as a shadow against the wall, its mouth with pointed teeth opening wide to swallow her whole, scythe in hand. Chills ran up Téa's arms, leaving little bumps in their wake. She rubbed her exposed forearms for warmth and tried to shake off the feeling of doom, "What do mean, evacuate earth? How is that even possible?"

The kitchen chair scraped against the floor as Florence scooted forward to lean on the table. "You yourself once teleported hundreds of people in a blink of an eye-"

Téa trembled in disbelief and stood swiftly. "That was completely different! That was only a couple hundred people, I only had to send them from the moon to Earth- and I just had my powers activated- I had an enormous burst of strength- I don't know that I could *ever* recreate that, let alone *the entire population of Earth*, are you insane?"

Téa was becoming increasingly irate as Florence watched her pace around the room in silence. "Well? Say something! How is this impossible plan even remotely possible!?"

Florence cleared her throat. "Are you quite done having your little freak-out?"

Téa *almost* growled and glared at her. "And how did you want me to respond Florence, calm, cool, and collected? How do you expect a normal person to react when they're told a mass planet-wide evacuation is supposed to happen in *three* days- or else be blown to smithereens- oh and that the fate of the world rests on your shoulders!?"

Florence took a deep breath and gestured to the empty seat for Téa to sit back down. Téa reluctantly took her place and allowed Florence to speak.

"First of all, please don't call me insane, it's rude. Secondly, the fate of the world does not rest on your shoulders. You will not be alone this time. Finally, would you like some tea, dear? Some toast? You look famished, and you haven't touched your coffee."

Téa stared at her incredulously. "Tea? Toast? Really?"

Florence stood quietly waiting.

Sheepishly, Téa said. "Um, yeah, actually that sounds nice."

Florence busied herself in the kitchen, giving Téa a moment to gather herself. Unable to keep her thoughts inside, she continued her tirade. "Also, how am I supposed to believe you? You. Of all people, how am I supposed to trust you with something so massively important?"

Florence sighed. "Maybe I didn't make myself clear, so I'll say it again. When I look into the future, each minute costs me one entire year of my life. I didn't figure it out until my sixth minute, but I sacrificed four additional years of my life looking into the depths of what's to come. Frankly, I'm not willing to waste another year of my life, giving you the proof that you seek. But I understand you need something. Ian has the proof. You can speak with him if you need something more to believe in me."

Tingles ran up and down Téa's body with a cold chill and she ground her teeth. "Ian knows?"

Florence shook her head. "Not exactly, I haven't told him about the whole world, you know..." She made a gesture of an explosion with her hands, eyes wide, and cheeks puffed out. "But I've given him other means of proof. I was waiting for your and Elijah's arrival before revealing it all."

Téa was quiet as Florence brought her tea and sat back down. "Which, by the way, you were cutting it pretty close. The big picture of the world's demise has never changed in any of my visions. But our success has been about fifty-fifty, and I was expecting you two days ago."

Téa choked on her drink and sputtered. "What? You mean, whatever your crazy ass plan is, you don't even know if it will work?"

Florence raised a placating hand. "A plan, no matter how crazy, is still a plan. It's our only chance for survival."

Téa took a deep breath and tried to calm her shaking hands. Her head spun, and she suddenly felt as though she might be sick. She pushed down the feeling and tried to gather herself. "So, what exactly is the plan?"

Florence crossed her legs where she sat and brushed the front of her shirt. "Have you ever heard of the collective conscious?"

Téa crinkled her nose as though she had just stepped into a giant cow patty in the middle of an abandoned field. "You mean like herd mentality? Have you been working with cult leaders, Florence?"

Florence stood, finally seeming to lose her patience with Téa's disbelief. "No. Think of it more like a collective force, like a string of energy connecting every living thing on this planet."

Téa laughed out loud. "Okay, so we're going to save the planet using fictional theories, great."

Florence slammed a palm on the table. "Enough Téa! You must start taking this seriously, it's not as though we have a lot of time to pull this off!"

Téa stiffened, but she resisted the urge to shout back. "Florence do not shout at me. I will listen, but you lost my respect a long time ago."

The two women sat at the table for a second of mutual stubborn annoyance before Florence continued. "Now, whatever you want to call it, all supernaturals have exhibited an outpouring of energy that has been flowing into a specific frequency in our world. Kind of like a radio frequency that is being powered by people with abilities. But it's a channel that is only shared by people who possess a Connex gene, and it's very difficult to tap into."

Florence was quiet for far too long, and Téa's annoyance slipped again. "I'm still listening."

Florence took another breath. "I know. It's just that this next part is difficult to explain, you must keep an open mind."

Téa held two fingers across her chest. "Scouts honor."

Florence huffed. "You were never a Girl Scout."

Téa clenched her jaw. "Are you going to tell me or not!?"

Florence calmly put her cup down perhaps a little too forcibly, but continued to speak. "Souls in the other realm can tap into it easily, and those souls who still have mates alive on Earth can connect that energy to their matches, loop the energy back in instead of flowing out."

Téa's blood rushed through her veins. "Wait, you mean soulmates?"

"Not just soulmates, anyone who possesses a Connex gene, and has had a loved one who has died can be threaded into this energy field."

Téa felt a great deep pit grow in her stomach. "Great, so we just need someone who can talk to the dead, to what- send out a memo to the passed souls and tell them to connect this energy to any Connex person still alive on Earth? Then what do we do with that energy, Florence? Stop the meteor? Do we teleport? Where to? I blew up the space station. Last I checked, we haven't discovered another habitable planet. Maybe Mars but with a shit-ton of work, resources, and time that we simply don't have."

For the first time Florence seemed panicked. "Wait- have you not connected with Annabelle yet?"

The old familiar heartache wormed its way through Téa's chest. "You mean my dead sister? No, we haven't exactly *chatted*, Florence."

Florence tapped her fingers on the table and bounced a leg up and down. "Damn it! Why did you have to get here so late! Téa, you must let Annabelle in, you can't tell me that you haven't sensed her at all? That she hasn't tried to reach out to you? Maybe through a dream? Anything?"

Téa felt the blood drain from her face, she sat at the table probably white as a ghost as she said. "There was a dream, more of a nightmare. She tried to warn me of something coming. We were on the space station when the moon cracked in half, sending us flying, exploding everything before I woke up... and in the miner's tunnel, I- accessed my full powers again, not just manipulation of metal and strength, but all of it."

The old woman was now the one pacing. "Good, good, okay so you're getting close. Téa, you have the strongest Connex powers we have ever seen. You are the key to connecting everyone with abilities. Also, you must let Annabelle in. She knows where the new planet is."

It was almost too much, Téa's knees went weak, she struggled to keep herself from collapsing. "New planet? Are you joking? What new planet? Is it like ours? Is there an advanced society? Medicine? Technology? Are we starting from scratch?"

Florence stopped her pacing and put her hands on Téa's shoulders. "Pull it together." The old woman hesitated and dropped her hands. "And I don't know. I don't know everything, Téa. I just know that Annabelle has a destination. Also, we can't stop the meteor, we tried that and we failed."

A desperate laugh escaped Téa's lungs. "So I'm supposed to connect all supernaturals to each other. Their deceased loved ones will then connect them to the energy field—and who exactly do you know who can talk to the dead to coordinate all these souls?"

"Not someone that I know. Someone that *you* know. Elijah can talk to the dead. He can coordinate them."

The truth smacked Téa in the face sobering her to her core. She knew it to be true. Elijah had talked to Annabelle. "My God Florence, you can't put the weight of this on that kid's shoulders. He's already lost his parents. This is all too elaborate. There has to be another way. Storm shelters—we'll send out an emergency broadcast—"

"NO! Stop grasping for straws and listen to me! There is no other way that the human race survives. What's coming to hit the moon is bigger than Titan."

Téa felt the bile rise in her throat and swallowed it back. "Titan? Like Saturn's biggest moon? What's coming is bigger than Titan?"

"Yes."

Téa walked away from the kitchen area, plopped onto the couch, and buried her head in her hands, completely drained of any remaining emotion other than fear and defeat.

She slowly raised her head and looked at Florence. "Three days?"

Florence sat on the couch next to Téa and patted her knee. "Yes dear, three days."

Téa and Florence walked side by side back to Ian's house in silence. Despair settled itself around, and inside her like a snake coiling around all her innards and squeezing tight. *The birds, we just got them back.* She couldn't stop thinking of all the things she would miss, *if* they even managed to succeed, down to the leaves crunching under her feet. Then she thought of Celia. Her plump little hands, her sparkling eyes just like her father's, the squeal she makes whenever she gets excited. If there was a chance her daughter could have a future, they had to try.

She paused in front of Ian's door and took a deep breath. She slowly turned the knob and took that first step into the next chapter of their lives as she passed through the threshold.

"Oh my God Téa!" Emma rushed towards her and enveloped her into a giant hug with her very pregnant belly pushing into Téa's own empty space. "We were just about to send out a Sanctuary wide alert, Ian is beside himself. Zephyr is the only one who stayed calm, something about trusting you to take care of yourself, they'll be so relieved!"

Emma flittered back down the hallway and shouted. "She's back! Call off the search!"

As Emma's bare footsteps sounded further away, Florence looked at her. "Are you ready?"

Téa straightened her shoulders. "We have to be."

Téa heard Celia's cry before she saw her. Zephyr hurried towards them and wrapped one arm tightly around her as he held their daughter with the other. "I'm so glad you're back. I knew you'd be okay. Although I must not have been as calm on the inside, Celia can feel my emotions too. She's been whimpering all morning. We missed you."

Guilt misted over her in a thin veil, but the problems they were about to face caused anxiety and fear to tear around inside her overpowering the guilt. "I'm sorry I worried you all. I wasn't anticipating being gone so long. We all have a lot to talk about."

Téa watched Zephyr, who was clearly hesitant to say whatever it was that he was going to say next. Finally, he cleared his throat. "Um, could you feed Celia first? We were just about to head to the supply storages for some formula, but I think she'd prefer your milk."

Her guilt grew thicker for having not realized that Celia was at least an hour late for her next feeding, but Téa plastered on a smile. "Of course. Come here, baby girl."

Téa's heart warmed when their daughter willingly went to her arms. She tried to hold back the wave of tears that wanted to spill over. She was glad to have Zephyr back, she just hadn't realized the ache that would accompany the act of sharing her daughter, even if it was with Celia's father. If Téa was only to be used as a milkmaid, she'd take it, and any other moment she could steal back with her daughter.

After Celia's belly was full, Téa slowly made her way to the living room. Her legs were like two cement logs carrying her to the end of the hallway. She could hear the group chattering softly from the other side of the wall, even the faint sound of laughter. *Florence hasn't told them yet.*

When she rounded the corner, they all turned from where they sat, all eyes on her. Their pupils lasered into her, so full of unknowing innocence and expectancy for a simple explanation of her short-lived disappearance.

Téa cleared her throat and looked at Emma. "Um, there are some big things we all need to discuss, that you need to know about as well, but do you think you could take the kids somewhere for an hour or so? I'll fill you in when you get back."

The little guilt monster inside of Téa dug its nails into her sides in response to the look of worry that spread across Emma's face. But Téa was surprised when Emma said. "It sounds like whatever we need to talk about, you might not want to repeat. I trust my neighbor. She watches Nora all the time—I'm sure she wouldn't mind watching Celia and Elijah as well. Give me ten minutes?"

Knowing Emma, her best and only friend, would be at her side while she and Florence delivered the hardest news they would ever have to share. Téa smiled. "That sounds great. I'll get Celia's diaper bag."

When Emma returned from dropping off the children with her neighbor, the adults were all once again seated in the living room.

It was quiet. Téa gulped. "First, Ian, can you tell me why you trust Florence so much?"

Florence scoffed. "Really, still Téa, after everything-"

"Please, I need to hear it, Florence."

Florence held her tongue, and a crease formed between Ian's eyes before he replied. "I'm sure you know, but the Sanctuary doesn't have weather forecasting. Florence told us a big storm was coming, and that we would all be trapped inside our homes for about four days. I didn't believe her at first but decided there was no harm in being prepared. We boarded up windows, made sure people had enough firewood, medication in case anyone came down with a fever, food, water. Then the snow came. She was right. We were all snowed in for not just four, but six whole days. We never could have imagined that the storm would be so intense. We would have lost a lot of community members if it weren't for her." Ian was quiet for a minute then continued. "Also, she knew Emma was pregnant before we did. She could have kept quiet about the storm, Téa. She could have just saved herself, but she saved the baby, she saved all of us. I have no reason *not* to trust her."

Emma cleared her throat and looked at Téa. "You know what I went through. But what you have to understand is, Florence was the only one who was ever there for me. She kept Nora and me at her house all the time. Fed us, clothed us. Whether or not she could have stopped it, doesn't matter to me. All that matters is that she gave me and my baby a safe place to sleep at night. I hold no ill will towards her." Emma scooted closer to Téa on the couch and held her hands. "I trust her Téa."

Téa took in a deep cleansing breath, fingers trembling and heart heavy. "Something is coming for us. Something big."

Téa felt like she was being battered, each informational bomb she dropped ricocheted off them; Ian, Zephyr, and Emma, sending back hit after hit of sadness and fear. She felt crumpled, a piece of paper squeezed, never to be smoothed out again. When she had finally shared everything, poured herself out, she felt hollow, empty, and tired.

Zephyr was the first to talk afterward. "So, we need you and Elijah to harness your powers to pull this off?"

Téa was about to reply, but Florence cut her off. "Yes. But there's one more thing."

Téa shot Florence a glare, *how many more revelations was the old hag hiding?*

"We don't have as much time as I was hoping for. I don't believe that we can save all the inhabitants of Earth. I believe that our only chance at success is gathering every person who has abilities, bring them here, and together we teleport the Sanctuary. Not just the people, but the whole Sanctuary, structures, dirt, and all. So that we have medical equipment," Florence nodded at Emma's swollen belly, "and food, seeds, dirt, shelter. We don't know what this new planet will be like. Not until Téa connects with Annabelle again, and we can't know for sure when that will happen. We need to prepare for the worst. We have three days to gather as many supernaturals as possible. We'll send the word out to as many communities as we can. We'll keep it discreet and tell them only that we need assistance from anyone with abilities. We cannot create a worldwide panic. We'll be swarmed. The world cannot know."

Téa couldn't hold it back any longer, the nauseous feeling that had been building up overcame her. She rushed to the bathroom and let out the sick. Grabbing the porcelain for stability, letting it all release. The Earth was going to die. It was the first time it had really sunk in. The full reality of what was to come. The lives that would be lost. The animals, plants, flowers, art, history. They had salvaged so much in the past months for nothing. It was all for nothing.

After Téa's stomach was empty and her mind numbed from the emotional pain, she walked back to the living room. Emma was crying on Ian's shoulder. Then Zephyr looked at her.

She wanted to collapse into his arms and forget about everything. Let his warmth chase away the darkness. But the awkwardness from the night before still lingered and kept her still. And when he made the first move and enveloped her in his embrace, the tears finally came. Taking with them their earthly sins as they fell.

Chapter Twenty
Zephyr

The room and everyone in it fell away when he looked into her eyes. It didn't matter what had happened, or what was about to happen. All that mattered was her. He swiftly walked over to Téa and wrapped his arms around her, and Téa cried against him, he knew that he would do whatever he could to keep her safe, to keep his family safe.

He was about to tell her how much she meant to him when she stiffened and pulled away. "Oh my God, Angie and William, I need to call them, they need to get here. And Eleanor, I haven't heard from her. She was supposed to be back from her trip to the East coast the same day you and Elijah showed up. I need to find her Zephyr; I can't leave them."

A new wave of sobs poured out of her as he held on tight. He gently tugged her chin up to look into her eyes and said. "We'll do everything we can to find her. I promise. And we can go call William right now. Sandstone has a telephone, and I'm sure the Sanctuary does as well right, Ian?"

Ian looked up from where he was holding Emma and nodded. "Yes, of course, it was one of the first places we got telecommunication set back up."

Looking at Ian holding Emma, and knowing how much his own family meant to him, a thought occurred to Zephyr. "Florence, at some point these supernaturals will need to know what's happening in order to help us, is that right?"

Florence nodded her head and Zephyr continued. "If we lure people with abilities here under false pretenses, and after they arrive tell them the world is ending, I'm going to guess that a lot of them won't be willing to leave their families behind, they won't help us. And besides that, I'm guessing we'll need all the help we can get, supernatural or not, once we arrive on the new planet. I think we need to bring their families too."

Florence crossed her arms, a woman made of stone, an immovable force. "Don't you all get it!? We must move fast; we must start reaching out right now so that people can make the trip from across the continent. How much time will be wasted when they have to pack up their families too? How much more difficult will it be to have multiple people travel versus one. Having them bring their families will only slow us down." She took a deep breath and flung her hands to the air. "And then there's the matter of getting additional people teleported to the new planet, have you any idea the energy it's going to take to transport the people already here in the Sanctuary, let alone adding more people?"

Zephyr ground his teeth; anger radiated off him like a heatwave. He moved away from Téa to face Florence; he stared her down before saying a single word. When he finally saw Florence's resolve turn hesitant, he spoke slow and firm. "Their *families* are coming, *and* we will save as many as we can, *regardless* of their abilities or lack thereof. The new planet will not be built by shoving others into the dirt. Enough of humanity is being demolished. If supernaturals are coming to help us, we will give them full disclosure."

Florence's eyes welled with unshed tears of anger. "Grandson, you're making a mistake, we will be over-run and our plan will fail."

Zephyr loomed over the frail old woman, but his tense muscles slackened at the mention of being called grandson. "What did you just call me? You're-my grandmother?"

Before anyone could reply Zephyr shook his head and kept talking. "The General's mother? That makes so much sense! No wonder your thought process is so wicked." His last words came out a growl. "Don't call me grandson, that man was never my father."

Florence softened, her muscles relaxed her face sad, and took a step towards him, but Zephyr pulled back. She relaxed her arms at her side and spoke to him more gently than he was prepared for. "You're right, that man was never your father, biologically or otherwise, and I was not that man's mother. I'm your *maternal* grandmother. You're right about one thing though. He is the reason I am the way I am now. I had to survive the General, survive him taking my daughter, and my unborn grandchildren for himself. If I could make it through that, then I will survive this apocalypse as well." Florence spun around and glared at Téa. "How have you not told him all of this!? Why is he still in the dark!?"

Zephyr put himself in between Florence and Téa. "Do not speak to her that way, grandmother or not. Téa and I haven't exactly had a lot of time together, yet she managed to caringly break the news that the man whom I thought to be my father was also my attempted murderer. She introduced me to my daughter, told me that I have a brother. She did all of that while bracing against the storm that seems to have followed us every step of our journey together-and for most of that time, I didn't even know who I was. I don't blame Téa; I admire her for her strength and determination to keep moving forward."

Silence sat heavy in the air.

Ian cleared his throat from across the room. "Right. Well, if we can get back to the matter at hand and save the family squabble for later, we don't exactly have a lot of time to spare."

Zephyr wanted to turn around and punch Ian right in the jaw, again. But he held his frustrations back and nodded. "Where do we start?"

Florence projected an air of confidence and supreme authority as she announced. "I have kept a list of all supernatural persons known to Dunamis and the resistance. We start by contacting the leaders of every former resistance group and give them the names of people who live in that territory and explain that we need their assistance urgently. Then we hold our breath that enough of them contact us."

Zephyr, his military preparedness kicking in, took back control of the room. "Florence can start making the phone calls and working the radio. In the meantime... Ian, I think you should take a handful of people and go out on a supply run. Stock up on as many supplies as you possibly can. We have to assume that we'll be starting from scratch on this new planet. Medical supplies, clean water, and shelf-stable food should be of the highest importance. Emma, can you help watch Celia for us? I'd like to train with Elijah and Téa."

Emma sniffled one last time and wiped her eyes, then nodded her head. "Yes, of course, however I can help."

Zephyr felt the warmth of Téa's body as she leaned against him and laid her head on his shoulder. "I'd like to contact Angie and William quickly before Florence starts her calls."

He planted a kiss on her temple and pulled her close. "Of course, I'll come with you."

Zephyr was seeing the Sanctuary for the first time with fresh eyes. His first and only other visit was entirely spent recovering in the hospital and then escaping with Téa under the cover of darkness. Everywhere he looked he saw happiness. Everyday simplicities of what he imagined a normal life could be. The sun shining down through the treetops created dancing puddles of light, shimmering their song for his delight.

He squeezed Téa's hand as they walked. "So this is going to be our new home huh? Granted it'll be situated on another planet, but it's not bad." He smiled and winked but was disheartened at her downcast expression. He nudged her shoulder and smiled some more. "Hey, as long as we're together everything will be okay, we can survive this."

She finally looked at him with those deep brown eyes so full of emotion it took his breath away. But her smile did not reach her eyes and there was a heaviness in his heart when her voice came out as a melancholy tune. "I just feel like the world is trying to drown me, Zephyr. I can't seem to catch up. I feel like the fate of humanity is resting on my shoulders and I don't know if I'll be able to pull this off."

Her pain made him ache to heal every broken thing for her. It was such a helpless feeling, not being able to fix everything. "I want to tell you that everything will be okay, but you and I both know that we can't say for certain that it will be. But what I can promise you, Téa, is that I will be here with you, every step of the way, you are not alone, and this isn't all on your shoulders. We'll fight through this together."

She was quiet after that, and he wished desperately that one of his powers could be mind reading. To see the world through her eyes and anticipate her needs, what a gift that would be. When they finally reached the communications center Téa picked up the pace and he hurried to stay by her side.

Zephyr fidgeted in his seat by Téa's side as she called Sandstone. Someone answered within seconds, and he figured out quickly that it was William on the other end. He listened to her end of the conversation and gathered a majority of what they were saying. Then watching Téa crumble all over again shattered his heart. Angie didn't simply faint back at Sandstone. She was unconscious for far too long. A catastrophic heart episode is what William had told Téa, Angie would never wake again, and William would not leave her. He would be content to live his final days by her grave and die a fulfilled man. Watching Téa's tears spill out of her almost broke Zephyr, but he wanted to be strong for her, for their daughter, and for Elijah. So, he wrapped his arms around her again and held on tight.

When her tears finally slowed and her breathing evened out, they made their way back to Ian's house. It was time to pick up Elijah and begin their training, three days would pass by quickly, and they had to master their abilities, the fate of humanity depended on it.

Chapter Twenty-One
Téa

Outside the communications center, the Sanctuary was bustling with activity. As they made their way back to Ian's house their path crossed with Florence's. She was on her way to the Vida Brigade, just outside the Sanctuary boundary, to begin radioing the leaders of the former resistance groups. When the General's men had been held accountable for their crimes, it left a lot of holes in the Dunamis system that needed filling. The resistance leaders were perfect to fill in the gaps. They were already trusted by their communities and knew how to lead.

Téa swallowed her pride for the sake of her aunt and forced out a smile as the old woman approached. "Hey Florence, can I talk to you for just a second?"

Florence rolled her eyes and crossed her arms. "Of course dear, not like I'm in a hurry trying to save the planet or anything."

Téa wanted to smack the fake smile off Florence's smug face, but clenched her hands tightly and took a deep breath. I just got off the phone with William at Sandstone. He hasn't heard from Eleanor. She's my aunt."

An awkward pause filled the space between them.

Florence tapped her toe. "...annnd?"

Téa ground her teeth and pushed down the scream that wanted to spill forth from her lungs. "*And,* she was due back from a trip to the east coast days ago. I was wondering if you might ask around about her while you're reaching out to the different leaders. I'm worried about her. She was going into an area that was rumored to still have heavy loyalist activity."

Finally, an ounce of humanity seemed to creep its way into Florence as concern curved her brow. "Yes dear, I can do that. I'll let you know if I hear anything. Why don't you and Zephyr head back to the computer lab and pick up a walkie-talkie, switch it to channel five, and I'll be able to reach you that way."

Téa surprised herself as her arms wrapped kindly around the old woman, an involuntary impulse of thanks and gratitude. Living a life of almost no affection made Téa overly appreciative of the smallest of kindnesses, and she was wound up tight in fear after hearing the news about Angie and knowing that Eleanor was still missing. Florence was stiff in Téa's embrace and the two women pulled away quickly. Téa shook her head as if clearing away the madness that momentarily overtook her, cleared her throat, and said. "Thanks."

Florence said nothing in reply and continued on her way sparing a confused glance behind her as she went.

Téa grabbed Zephyr's hand and he gave her a reassuring squeeze before he said. "Well, let's turn back around and grab that walkie-talkie, I'm sure the kids are still fine with Emma, it's only been what? Thirty minutes at most?"

She loved how naturally Zephyr stepped into the role of being a dad, always thinking of the kids and their needs. Then there was the way he always seemed to be able to read her- mind, body, and soul, so very aware of her in the most caring of ways. No matter what was happening around them, just being near him put her naturally anxious state at ease. Even with the danger that seemed to follow them, she had a sense of safety and calm when he was by her side.

Lost in thought, Téa realized Zephyr was nudging her arm. "He's not wrong you know." Zephyr said with a wink.

Téa had no idea what he was talking about. "I'm sorry, who's not wrong about what?"

Zephyr let out a hearty chuckle and wiped a tear from one eye as he kept laughing and they kept walking hand in hand. "You really didn't notice any of that, did you?"

Téa was tired and did not have the energy for whatever guessing game this was. "Zephyr, please, if it's not impor-tant-"

He turned and stopped directly in front of her, and pulled Téa close, both arms wrapped low around her waist and leaning back to look into her eyes. Then he spoke softly.

"There was a gorgeously handsome rock mountain size of a man," Zephyr paused then laughed and said sarcastically, "not that I'd know what constitutes as handsome these days," he said with a wink, "but he was ogling you from head to toe and made a gloriously inappropriate comment about your beauty and your body, and I have to say I agree. Although, I wouldn't necessarily be as vulgar as that." He finished by waving a hand to the side as though the man's words were dirt that polluted their air and he was trying to wave them away from the safety of their personal bubble. He stood still in front of her, those firm hands holding her close and smiled ear to ear.

Wait, was that a compliment? Is he flirting with me?

Téa didn't know what she was supposed to say, she didn't see or hear any other man, she had bigger things to worry about, and besides, she only had eyes for Zephyr. Wait... why were her arms like jello? Did her hands feel weird? What was this warm fluttering in her stomach? That smile of his was turning her to mush. She knew without a doubt she was in love with Zephyr, but she didn't know what to do with those feelings, or how to act. She was in a constant struggle between uncertainty and following her emotions blindly. Growing up the way she did, in the isolation that came with a captive military life, her relationship knowledge was essentially non-existent and came only from instinct. This back-and-forth banter was not something she knew how to do. What was *normal*?

After an uncomfortable silence, Zephyr dropped his arms from around her and gently pulled her forward to continue their walk. When they arrived back at the computer lab,

Zephyr wandered towards the closest desktop and woke it up while Téa browsed the shelving for a fully charged walkie-talkie. She paused her searching when a song floated to her ears.

What's Lost can always be found again

A happiness fluttered inside of her. Out of all the new things she had gotten the chance to experience with her newfound freedom, music was her favorite. Sure, movies were great, William's obsession with sci-fi had her watching entire series on Blu Ray, but music was unparalleled. She knew she was lucky to be the inheritor of Sandstone Estate. It provided her with the luxury of human comforts that were not readily available yet to the general public. Téa turned around and smiled. "I've heard this song before! How did you find music?"

Zephyr's eyes shone bright, those white teeth flashing at her as he grinned. "There's a whole playlist here, hundreds of songs. Ian mentioned something about Sanctuary celebrations, and I hoped... well, it was a lucky guess. Dance with me?"

The nervous wings of anticipation were smothered by the excitement of learning something new, surely, they could spare a few minutes for sanity's sake? "Absolutely, I would love to dance with you."

He held his arms open wide and she slowly walked up close to him. "Just follow my lead." Zephyr placed one of her hands on his shoulder and the other in his palm. His other arm rested gently around her waist, and then, they were gliding.

> *Real love darlin,*
> *Is a treasure that can never be taken*

Téa couldn't recall a single moment where she felt this kind of joy. The birth of Celia was of course a momentous event, but that was a different kind of happiness. Here and now, moving along with Zephyr she felt whole again. Like there had been a piece of her missing and he had brought it back from the void with him.

Zephyr slowed their movements and looked deep into her eyes. "Téa, I..." he hesitated, and she saw a lump in his throat bobbing up and down before he continued. "Before, that night we shared, after I asked you if you wanted to be with me, I didn't give you the space or time to answer." Unshed tears balanced on the rim of his eyes. "The way we were put together, arranged. I know without a doubt that regardless of how we met, you are the one for me. But now that we're here in this moment, I- " He swallowed and looked to the ground. "You've had your freedom these past months, and-well, I don't want you to feel like you have to be with me because of Celia or because I'm back. Please don't feel like you have to say anything right now, I just wanted you to know how I feel, and that I would never take your freedom away from you."

> *Follow me,*
> *I'll guide your trusting hand,*

To a better land,
Where freedom rings,
To cry is to deny the sand,
That would hold down our love,
With you I can fly,
Let's take to the sky,
So grab my wing,
To soar is to tour the corners of your heart,
Let's us glide,

As the music played in the background the room seemed to blur around him, Zephyr was all she saw. Standing so close together, the feel of his heart racing against her chest, the sweet mint scent of his breath on her nose, the way his hair fell just a bit into his gray eyes. There was only him. Only ever him.

Téa stopped their dancing and held his gaze. "Zephyr, I meant it when I said I love you. I didn't say it because I missed you, or because you're Celia's father, or even because I felt like I had to. I said it because I meant it. You are the one for me. Always and forever, *my* Zephyr. Please don't ever pull away from me. I might sink without you. Not because I rely on you, but because you are half of me. You have my heart Zephyr and without you, I'm not alive."

His tears finally spilled over, silent sobs creating waves between their bodies when he hugged her close. He hid his face in the elegant curve of her neck and pulled their bodies even tighter together. A new song started, and they began to dance again.

With you I am weightless,
Where love is found underground,
And life is a blessing,
No longer a tool,
To be valued

A weight melted away and Téa felt lighter than she ever had in her entire life, as though pure sunshine poured straight through her and lifted her into the air light as a feather.

When by your side,
Never blind,
Beauty,
Seeing all,
For what the future can hold,

They continued to move, and Zephyr looked at her with a renewed sort of delight, soft and sultry. His voice was husky when he asked her. "Téa, do you want to be with me?"

Instead of responding she placed her lips on his for just a moment tasting the sweetness of him and pulled away smiling.

He leaned in close and whispered in her ear. "I need to hear you say it."

Electricity shot up her sides and she wanted nothing more than to never let him go. "Yes, I want you Zephyr, to be with you in any and every way."

He laughed and stepped out then twirled her around. She squealed in gleeful excitement and eased into absolute peace when he twirled her right into his arms, her back to his chest. He placed his chin on top of her head, and she could feel him breathing her in. A new song started...

Heart racing,
All the time,
Seeing all with more than eyes,
Your heart belongs with mine,
Always fine,
By your Loving side,
Darling,
The world is mine,
Only,
When you are fine,
I'm okay,

Zephyr leaned close and whispered again. "You know, I didn't think I'd ever need this at the time, but a nurse at the hospital had given me this. She said Dunamis didn't control those types of things anymore and we were responsible for it ourselves now." He reached into his back pocket and pulled a condom out of his wallet. He kissed her cheek and whispered again as his hips swayed against hers. "Would you like to use it?"

Téa slowly spun around, looked up, heart pounding, a lioness racing inside her. "Yes. Please." She replied as she bit her lower lip.

Can conquer all,
win together,

I carry you with me,
Always,
What's found,
Can never be lost.

Gone was the hurt, the fear, the uncertainty of their futures. Téa only felt him, only saw him, only smelled him, the lilac and fresh cut grass scent that seemed to be permanently seeped into his pores so pleasantly. The future did not matter in this moment. Her lips, her body, hungry for his. Zephyr was all she could ever want or need. His touch, his voice, his laugh, his strength. In this moment, she was home again.

Chapter Twenty-Two

Téa

As they walked hand in hand back to their children Téas' heart fluttered, and her face hurt from grinning so much. It was hard not to feel content, happy, and complete by Zephyr's side, but she knew what she would soon have to face, and the tension and fear were creeping their way back in.

The golden light filtering through the treetops suddenly seemed heavy and sad. The excited shrieks from children turned ominous. Every crunching leaf or snapping twig was like a gunshot to her ears. She could not lose him, could not watch her daughter's life cut short. They had to pull this off.

Zephyrs' deep soothing voice cut through her thoughts like a pensive reprieve, saving her again from slipping down the rabbit hole of doom. "Hey, where'd you go?"

God, those pure gray eyes, his strong warm hand in hers, the feel of his body nudging against hers as they walked, her safe place.

She softly laughed. "I'm here, just lost in thought. You've known Elijah for a while now. Do you think he'll be able to do it? Reach out to hundreds of souls in three days?"

That kind chuckle, the fine lines at the corner of his eyes, she could drink him in for an eternity.

He dropped her hand and draped his arm around her shoulders then kissed the side of her head before responding. "You know, that kid has got to be the strongest person I have ever met. The way he handled losing his parents so suddenly and violently the way that he did, and what happened to us on the road... For him to come out the other side still making sarcastic jokes and fighting to keep up with the rest of us, well... Yes, I think he can do it."

Téa could feel his next question before it even left his lips, he hesitated but asked anyway. "What about you? How are you feeling about connecting to Annabelle? Can I do anything to help?"

She wrapped her arm around his waist as they walked and nuzzled into his side. "You already have." Genuine happiness chased away the shadows. "You found me, I feel alive again, and if it's possible to connect with Annabelle, to give me full and not just partial access to my soulmate powers, then you have definitely given me my best chance at having the strength to succeed."

Zephyr flashed her another of his dazzling smiles. "Well, that is some compliment. I believe in you, my sea star." He said with a wink and another kiss on the head.

Ian's house came into view and Emma was outside cradling Celia atop her very pregnant belly while Elijah played with Nora. Emma saw them approaching and waved, then shouted out to them. "Perfect timing!" She danced in place as though she were doing a little dance and reached out for Téa to take Celia. "I have to pee!" Téa took hold of her baby and Emma shot off.

Téa looked up at Zephyr and giggled. "I don't miss that, although I do have to cross my legs when I sneeze, wonder if that will ever go away?" She said rhetorically with a far-away look in her eyes.

Zephyr smiled and went over to Elijah. "How's it going little man?"

Elijah accepted Zephyr's help to stand from where he was sitting on the ground across from Nora having a tea party. He struggled to his feet and Zephyr handed him his crutches, then Elijah said. "I'm great! Just waiting for all you grown-ups to catch up."

Zephyr laughed. "What do you mean by that?"

Elijah let out an exaggerated breath and turned to face him. "Well, I've already been talking to a lot of souls, the real problem is the dark shadows."

Téa overheard their conversation and frowned. "Wait, Elijah what do mean dark shadows?" The hairs on Téa's neck stood up, she hugged Celia tighter, and her pulse started to race.

"Well, just like good people and bad people, there's good souls and bad souls. The bad souls look like blobby shadows." Elijah said it as though it was the most obvious thing in the whole world.

Zephyr leaned forward to be eye level with the boy. "Elijah, why are the dark shadows the real problem?"

Elijah shrugged like it was no big deal. "The dark shadows are trying to eat the bright souls. They're chasing them."

Téa's blood ran cold, her feet were frozen in place.

Elijah kept talking. "I showed the good souls where to hide, but the dark shadows are getting closer, it's getting hard to talk to new ones, the bad guys keep following me."

The world started to spin, and Téa's head felt light. She could hear Zephyr talking to her from far away as though she were underwater. She shook her head, and the world around her moved in slow motion, now was not the time to faint. "I think I need some water and something to eat." She said quietly.

Zephyr held onto her elbow to keep her steady as she held Celia. Téa looked behind her, "Come on Nora, let's go get some lunch." The little girl wobbled to her feet, and they all went inside.

Emma saw them all coming in and hurriedly waddled her way down the hall. "Téa? Are you okay? You look a little green."

Téa couldn't respond, she felt nauseous, and Zephyr guided her into the kitchen and pulled out a chair for her to sit down. "Do you want me to take Celia?" She nodded her head and carefully passed their baby into his arms.

The kitchen and dining areas were open to the living room and Téa saw Emma pull open a cabinet door against one wall and bring out sheets of paper and crayons. She set Nora down with the colors then joined Téa, Zephyr, and Elijah at the table.

Zephyr spoke first. "Elijah just informed us that there are dark souls fighting the light souls, and they're making it difficult for him to reach more good souls."

Emma, with a sharp intake of breath, placed her hand over her mouth, eyes wide. "What are we going to do? How can we even fight that?"

Elijah's lip quivered and Téa remembered that despite his nonchalant attitude, he was still an eight-year-old boy. She willed her mind to focus, she needed to be strong now. She reached a hand across the table towards him, looked him in the eyes, and with a calm kind voice said. "Hey kiddo, it's going to be okay. You know my sister Annabelle, right?" He nodded his head and sniffled before she continued. "Well, I'm about to have a conversation with her." Téa sat up proudly and smiled. "She and I are going to figure out a way to kick those dark shadows right in the butt!"

Elijah laughed, such a sweet and innocent sound. "You said butt!" He kept laughing and Téa's heart felt lighter.

Zephyr spoke up then. "Hey little man, why don't you go color with Nora while we make you some lunch?"

Elijah scoffed. "Coloring is for babies."

Emma laughed and stood up. "Well, you are in luck because I also have some awesome colored pencils and a guidebook for drawing dinosaurs. Would you like that better."

Elijah's face lit up in joy and he nodded his head as Emma helped him over to the living room.

Téa leaned her head against Zephyr's front, he was seated in the chair next to hers. He was holding Celia who was fast asleep in the crook of one arm. Téa took deep slow breaths until she was calm enough to feel his heartbeat through his shirt. Then she whispered. "Things just got a lot more complicated, didn't they?"

He gently pulled her chin up and softly pressed his lips against hers. All air left her lungs and she held herself back from deepening the kiss. He nuzzled his nose against hers and leaned their foreheads together and she thought her beating chest might explode.

Then he whispered back. "You are stronger than you give yourself credit for. Besides, I'm up for a little challenge, bad souls, no big deal." He winked and she couldn't help herself, the laughs echoed out of her, and with them some of her fear, until she was gasping for air.

She wiped a tear from her eye and sat up. "Thanks, I needed that."

His voice was more serious when he replied. "Hey, I meant what I said, you're stronger than you give yourself credit for."

Téa felt the vise grip of tension ease and smiled. She got up and went to help Emma in the kitchen who was making everyone a lunch of sandwiches with homemade bread and fresh fruit from the gardens. When they were all almost done eating Téa felt a tug on her sleeve. She could see the worry in Emma's eyes. "Do you think Ian will be back in time from the supply run?"

Téa placed a tender hand on Emma's arm and nodded. "Of course. He'll be back early, *and* with enough supplies to sustain us for years. You know Ian, he's a 'Jack of all trades' he can handle anything that's thrown at him."

Emma smiled and got up to clear the table. Téa was about to offer to help when Celia made a small cry and wiggled in Zephyr's arms. She reached for her baby and cradled her, then lovingly said. "Hello sleeping beauty, you must be starving." Téa then looked to Zephyr. "I'm going to go change her and nurse her. Then if you'll watch her for a while, I think I'm going to go on a walk, try and clear my mind."

Zephyr smiled and nodded. "I'll be here when you're ready."

Téa made her way down the hall bouncing slightly and cooing to Celia, taking in every tiny finger, every expression in her small face, and her sweet baby smell. Téa's only goal in life was to protect her child. She needed to connect with Annabelle, and soon. She could see now how Elijah could not keep handling the souls alone. He needed help. Téa needed full access to her powers.

Time was running out.

Chapter Twenty-Three

Téa

After leaving Celia with Zephyr, Téa decided to walk to the fishpond. It was her favorite spot in the Sanctuary during her first visit here, and she hoped it was still there. She needed a place to focus, to calm her mind, and try to connect with her sister. As she walked along the various paths that snaked their way through the cabins and trees, she tried to clear her thoughts of all the negatives, all the 'what ifs'.

But a rush of anger overcame her. Why was saving humanity put on her shoulders? Why did she have to be chosen for a life of heartache and struggle? Loss after loss and battle after battle, that's all she had ever known. She could count on one hand her moments of happiness. That didn't seem like enough, it wasn't fair. None of her life was fair.

Téa forced her feet forward step after step, kept in motion by momentum, a zombie on autopilot. A flutter stirred inside her heart when she saw the opening to the dome that once housed the fishpond. *Please be there.* She walked inside and let out a sigh of relief. It was exactly as she remembered. Untouched by the confrontation with the General's men.

The oval-shaped room with a dirt floor and large rock pond in the center was completely empty of other people. The surface of the water glistened; it bounced back the small streams of light that crept towards it from the entrance. A small splash alerted Téa to the presence of the various scaled friends under the water, and it lit a small amount of hopefulness within her.

Téa sat down and crossed her legs. Took a deep breath and filled her lungs with damp earthen air. She let the mild sounds from the pool of water, that echoed around the dim room, surround her like a blanket. She immersed her thoughts with nothing more than Annabelle. The limited days they shared together mixed with her recovered memories of their childhood when their soulmate gene was previously activated. Everything she had of Annabelle, she pulled it forward. She ran her fingers over the smooth curve of the two golden wedding bands from their parents that she wore around her neck.

Téa four years old and Annabelle two years old, crawling into Téa's bed in the middle of the night. Barely able to lift her little toddler legs over the low bed rail. Snuggling in close holding her stuffed bunny tight.

Five-year-old Téa and three-year-old Annabelle getting into their mother's makeup. Taking turns using the soft bristles of a powder brush on each other's cheeks. Gently, carefully, and very clumsily spreading the soft crimson lipstick across each other's mouths. Giggling as they took turns walking in mommy's pretty shoes'.

Being reunited, eighteen-year-old Annabelle and twenty-year-old Téa, hugging. Embracing each other, and never wanting to let go.

Silent tears were streaming down Téas' cheeks. "I miss you, Sister."

"I'm here, I've always been here."

Téa gasped at hearing Annabelle's voice, clear as day, as though she were sitting right next to her.

"Annabelle?"

"Who were you expecting? Some magnificent goddess? Well, I mean I am that too you know. Yes, of course, it's me!! I've missed you too sister."

Téa laughed at Annabelle's humor, she sounded the same, as alive and full of life as the day she left her body. Her voice almost sang with warmth and joy.

"Now, what is the deal with all this self-pity? Why me? It's not fair. Blah blah blah. Shake out of it Téa! It's not just you. The whole world was broken for decades, and you have a whole team of people behind you, supporting you. Knock off the woe-is-me attitude and start fighting back!"

"I am fighting back! I've been fighting my whole life just to live!"

"*No. Stop it, Téa. Take a deep breath and think of all the good your life has had.*"

Images flashed in Téa's mind; memories supplied by Annabelle. The first time Zephyr held her hand. The first brush of his lips on hers. The first-time birdsong was returned to the earth. Celia's first toothless little smile and coo. Téa had blood coursing through her veins, a daughter, a family, love.

"You're right. I need to pull it together. I'm stronger than this."

"*Damn right you are!*"

Téa couldn't stop the laughter that jumped out of her, a hearty chuckle. "God, I really miss you." Her smile reached her eyes, she was feeling like herself again. "I wish I could see you."

"*You can if you try. Just focus. Téa, you started the link. You can feel the connection between us, right? Zero in on that and make it grow.*"

"Okay, I'll try."

"*That's right, you got this, you can rock it, girl!*"

Téa laughed again. "Annabelle, shh, I can't focus with all your cheerleading."

Téa quieted her mind and listened to the small splashes coming from the pond again. Soon the sound grew into waves crashing on the beach, blue skies filled her vision, and finally, electricity eased into her fingertips. The sparks were internal and small at first but grew to thunderbolts shooting up her arms until the energy wormed its way throughout her entire body. She vibrated with the strength of the power running through her, and at last, a sharp crack reverberated the ground around her. Téa was at full strength, her connection with Annabelle and her soulmate abilities vivid. Her old self was back, and better than before.

"Holy shit!"

"Holy shit!"

The girls laughed together, and when Téa turned around, she saw her sister. Annabelle was just as perfect as when she was alive. Straight long black hair, slender form, brown bright eyes, dimples in her cheeks. Happiness filled her face like a sunflower in full bloom.

"Oh my god, it's like you're alive. I could almost touch you."

Téa stood and reached out steadily towards Annabelle, but when her hand reached Annabelle's shoulder it went straight through her, a ghost.

Tears started to well within her.

"No, you stop that. This is a gift Téa, no tears. We have each other again."

Téa nodded her head, and pushed the heartbreak away. "You're right, this is a gift. I just thought, maybe, for a minute-"

"I know what you thought, but I'm still here."

The words wouldn't come, a lump in her throat stopped the flow of everything she wanted to say. Overcome with enormous gratitude at getting the chance to connect with Annabelle again. She was lucky and needed to start acting like it. Téa could only nod and smile, the beautiful sight of her sister permanently seared in her brain.

Their reunion was cut short by the sound of pounding footsteps outside the mouth of the semi-sphere. She heard heavy breathing before Florence's flushed face came into view.

The old woman was practically shouting at her. "There you are! I've been looking everywhere for you! Your Aunt Eleanor's been trying to reach you, she radioed Sandstone, and William told her you were here. She won't talk to anyone but you. We'll have to go to the Vida Brigade and radio her back."

Shock and excitement flooded Téa's body and she smiled wide at Annabelle.

Florence stared at Téa. "What are you looking at? Did you hear me? We found your aunt."

Laughing. "She can't see me Téa, only you and Elijah can. Come on, snap out of it, go see what your aunt has to say."

Téa narrowed her eyes at her sister's sly gaze, her sister knew something already, she was sure of it. "What aren't you telling me?"

Confusion overcame Florence's face. "What on earth are you talking about? Get it together, we must hurry."

Téa nodded and turned to follow Florence as they made their way out into the daylight. The sun was low in the sky. Already their first day was almost gone. Panic started to creep its way back into Téa's arsenal of emotions.

The smooth rock path clipped underfoot as Téa talked to Florence without looking at her, "Is my aunt okay? Is she injured? Where is she?"

Téa could sense the irritation radiating out through Florence and the old woman sighed before responding. "As I said, she'll only talk to you."

The hour walk to the Vida Brigade was torture. Moving side by side without talking, the silence squeezing Téa tight like a vise. She busied herself by counting every tree they passed as a mark of their progress. Her hearing heightened to every rustle of a bush, every squawk overhead, every chirruping of the grasshoppers talking from their hiding spots. A soft breeze blew through Téa's long curly hair and she shivered. She wished she had brought a sweater.

Finally, they reached the outskirts of the Sanctuary. The Vida Brigade had been updated since she last saw it. The airy aged treehouses above them looked abandoned. Five long concrete structures stretched out in front of them, illuminated with light from the small square windows that dotted their sides. The sun had finally set, and lampposts turned on automatically, they buzzed as Florence and Téa walked past the first building and into the second.

Inside there was one long hallway with half a dozen doors lining one side. Florence opened the first door and gestured for her to go in. Téa's skin crawled. She hated the feeling of being led willingly into a prison. But Florence needed Téa; she wasn't going to lock her up. She shook off the feeling and squinted into the darkness. Florence flipped the light switch and Téa blocked her eyes.

In front of them was a long table with three chairs and three radios.

Téa scrunched her nose in confusion. "If we have three radios, why are you the only one making calls? Time is of the essence you said. We should have others helping us."

Florence huffed in response and pulled a chair out to sit down. "It's kind of a sensitive subject, don't you think? We don't exactly want everyone knowing what's coming. We don't need a panic on our hands."

Téa was dumbfounded and crossed her arms. "Are you serious right now, Florence? It's literally the fate of humanity hanging in the balance. We need all the help we can get."

Téa saw Florence's shoulders curve slightly. Her voice was quieter when she replied. "I haven't had much luck with the leaders I've contacted so far. I've called ten. Half don't believe me, and the other half are going to try and fend for themselves."

That rush of anger was threatening to take Téa over again. "Damnit Florence!"

The old woman turned to face Téa, her own anger spilling out. "Don't you shout at me! I damn well know the implications of not receiving any assistance!"

Téa froze. A mixture of emotions collided inside her; annoyance, fear, denial. Florence turned the radio on, and it hummed to life, a red dot let her know it was ready. Florence switched to the right channel and spoke into the microphone. The old woman read out a string of numbers and letters, the Sanctuary call sign and waited.

It was only moments when someone spoke back.

"Hello? Hello? Yes, I'm here, this is Eleanor-"

Téa reached across Florence and pressed the talk button excitedly. "Eleanor!? Oh my God, where are you? It's me, Téa."

Florence scooted out of the way and let Téa take the chair in front of the radio. She sat down and allowed the enormous gust of relief to fill her as she listened to Eleanor's familiar and beautiful voice drift towards her.

"Téa? Thank goodness. I was so worried when William said you weren't there. What happened? Why did you leave?"

Téa laughed and wiped the tears of happiness away. "That's a long story. Listen, Auntie, I need you to come to the Sanctuary right away. Don't go home. Come straight here."

Eleanor's voice was shaky. "Wait, listen, darling. A lot has happened here... I have some people here who need help. Do you have any Dunamis contacts nearby?"

The panic was growing again. "I understand you'd like to help people, but... we don't have the time. I need you here the day after tomorrow. There are a handful of Dunamis outposts along the east coast, tell me where you are, and I'll direct you to the closest one."

A deep breath came through the microphone. "Listen, sweetheart, I can't leave right now. I found... I found Mabel. But I also found a loyalist compound. We were able to overtake them. But, well it's hard to explain. It seems the loyalists were rounding up people with Connex genes. They were experimenting on the boys. It's gruesome here. I need to get them out."

Téa's heart started to race. "Wait... did you say people with Connex genes? Oh my God Auntie that's amazing!" Her panic instantly drowned out with hope.

Eleanor's voice was full of confusion. "Sweetheart, did you hear what I said? The Loyalists were experimenting on them. We need help here, medical care, communication to get in touch with their families."

Guilt gnawed at Téa. These people had families and they didn't have time to reunite them. She steeled herself before saying her next words. "Eleanor, this is going to be difficult to hear and you might not believe me, but you must. You must trust me on this." Téa took a deep breath before pushing the talk button again. "The world is going to end, not sometime in the distant future, but the day after tomorrow. You have to leave, now. If you're still on the east coast, it's going to take almost every minute to get you all here in time. I need you to bring every person with abilities with you. I'll call ahead to the closest Dunamis outpost and get you set up with transportation for everyone, a doctor as well if they have one. I'll make sure there's food and water ready and waiting. But you must hurry."

It was quiet for what felt like an eternity before Eleanor finally replied. "The world is ending?"

Téa tried to keep her voice from shaking but failed. "Yes Auntie. But humanity has a chance to survive *if* we get enough supernatural's here in time to help. Where are you?"

Téa heard Eleanor clear her throat before talking again. "Um, we're somewhere in between Delaware and Maryland, close to St. Michaels."

Excitement permeated Téa's entire body. "That's perfect! There's a Dunamis outpost in Chesapeake Bay. It's only eighteen miles by boat or an hour and a half by driving. Do you have any means of transportation to get there?"

There was the sound of Eleanor pushing the talk button on the radio before she said. "Yes, I came here with a group of parents in boats looking for their children..." Téa heard Eleanor's voice catch before she kept talking. "They're all dead now, there should be enough space for all of us."

The guilt reared its ugly head again like a snake curling around Téa's heart. She cleared her throat before she replied. "I'm so sorry Auntie. I'll call the outpost and inform them of your pending arrival." Téa hesitated before continuing. "Listen, it's probably best to not tell them everything I told you. I'll tell you the rest when you get here, but just get here. Please, Auntie, we need you and all the help we can get if we're going to survive what's coming."

Téa's heart ached at the sorrow in Eleanor's voice. "I understand darling. We'll see you soon."

The radio went silent, and Téa dropped her head into her hands. Florence squeaked in excitement behind her and clapped her hands. "This is amazing! It's all going to work out!"

Téa could not hold back any longer, she stood up, turned around, and finally, she did smack the smile off Florence's face. The slapping sound of skin against skin filled the room and the sting of the strike burned her hand.

Téa's voice was menacing as she growled. "How dare you."

Florence cradled the spot where Téa hit her, mouth agape and frozen in place. She didn't say anything as Téa continued. "Celebrating when you heard everything. These children just survived torture. Their parents were murdered trying to save them. They get no time to heal, no time to grieve. And here you are jumping for joy."

Florence dropped her hand and straightened her stance, her jaw locked. "Don't you dare tell me you weren't excited too when you heard there were supernaturals there. Do you not get it? We are on the verge of extinction. We don't have the luxury of *emotions*. We only have tasks that need to be done, and this is one big task off our checklist." Florence crossed her arms tightly and said. "Why don't you just teleport them all here and save us some time and stress?"

Téa looked down. "I can't. I have to see the place the place they are being teleported from, and all the people, I need it like an anchor, otherwise I can't do it, no matter how much power I have."

Florence shook her head and said. "Well, that's a disappointment." Then she turned to leave.

Téa glared at Florence's back as the old woman left the room, leaving her to sit alone in silence. She hated the small part of her that knew that the old hag was right. What kind of new world were they starting? And did they deserve it? Téa wasn't so sure anymore.

Chapter Twenty-Four
Eleanor

A group of girls stood behind Eleanor as the glow from the radio dimmed and the sound went silent. Amber leaned over the swivel chair that Eleanor sat in and stood silently.

Mabel stood by Eleanor's side and rubbed her hand up and down Eleanor's arm. "So, the end of the world huh? I guess we'd better get a move on."

Eleanor spun the chair around and saw some of the younger girls crying. The older girls held back their own tears as they tried to calm them down. It seemed as though everything moved in slow motion as she made her way out of the small office. Steadily her senses came back to her bit by bit. Then she remembered, some of the girls had started to leave. The announcement—how many of them stayed?

Heart racing and legs pumping, she rushed through the dark dirt tunnels dimly lit by the string of light bulbs. She could hear footsteps behind her trying to keep up. She had to get to the exit and make sure no one else left. It was not only about needing their help, but now it was also about saving their lives.

Finally, she burst through and out into the forest night, and there they were. The rest of the supernaturals. Mostly girls, but a few boys as well, illuminated by the moon. There must have been a second room of boys who had not been cut to pieces yet. They were all kneeling on the ground, most were crying, some were pale and looked as though their feet could not hold them much longer.

Then Eleanor's eyes found the ground. The bodies had not been moved yet. The children were taking in the sight of their parents' unmoving forms, never to breathe again, laying still in the large clearing.

She dropped to her knees gasping for air. How was she going to do this? Tell them life as they knew it was going to cease to exist the day after tomorrow. Then convince them all to follow her to a place they had never been, *and* ask for their help? It was all so daunting, too much to ask of some who were so young. Right now, they needed comfort, protection, hope. She didn't know if she had it in her. But then she realized, they deserved a chance at a full life, and she could possibly give that to them. She couldn't let herself think of it as her asking *them* for help. She had to think of it as *her* getting them to safety. It was the only way.

When her pulse finally slowed, Eleanor rose and brushed the dirt off her pants. She cleared her throat and tried to project her voice as loud, kind, and calm as she could. "I know you all are hurting, and I know there are no words that can take away the pain you all have endured." She paused and then continued. "But there's a way out of all of this, a fresh start. There's a place, it's called the Sanctuary, where we can all go to be free, to be safe. Please, come with me and we can all begin to heal together."

One of the girls a few feet away sniffled and wiped her nose on her sleeve. "My dad is back in town. What if he's still alive? I want to go home." The girl, probably no older than ten, hiccupped as she talked.

Eleanor's heart hurt for the girl, for all of them. Her hands started to shake, and she held them together in front of her to stop the tremble. She didn't know how to tell the girl they didn't have time to get to her dad or bring her home. Leaving the girl here alone was out of the question. Lying was not in Eleanor's nature, but her years of being held prisoner and servant by the General had given her practice at putting on a brave face.

Eleanor bit her tongue and cleared herself of expression. "The town has been destroyed. I'm so sorry to have to tell you all, but there is no one left in St. Michaels."

A boy in the back perked up and shouted. "What about Wilmington? That's where they took me from, my mom's there!"

Nausea rolled around Eleanor's belly, worms wiggling inside of her. She hadn't thought the loyalists extended that far north. But the journey to the Sanctuary would take them northeast. They did not have time to go northwest.

Her heart in a vise grip and she told the next lie. "I'm devastated to tell you, but the loyalists have taken back control of the continent. They are everywhere. Where I am taking you is the only safe place left. After we're settled, we can begin rescuing anyone who may have relatives still alive."

Eleanor fought the urge to vomit. Was she doing the right thing? Maybe she should tell the truth? But what if they didn't believe her? The Earth ending was difficult for anyone to wrap their mind around. Then she looked behind her. Mabel, Amber, and the small group of girls who had already heard the news, the truth, were staring at her from the mouth of the tunnels. No one said a word, not even one of them contradicted her. They knew she was in an impossible position, why else stay silent?

She found the strength to continue talking to the large group of supernaturals outside. "Come with me. We have one last reliable Dunamis outpost. They will give us supplies to get to the Sanctuary. From there we can re-group."

The supernatural's started to nod and move towards Eleanor. She mustered up her courage and said one last thing. "We'll go make sure everyone is free from the tunnels. There are boats at the bottom of the cliff wall. We'll use those to get to the outpost. Then straight to the Sanctuary as quickly as we can."

The large group slowly walked back towards the tunnels to begin their search for survivors, and Eleanor rushed into a grouping of trees and emptied her stomach until she was dry heaving. Afterward, the sobs came, and she felt a gentle hand on her back. Eleanor wiped her mouth on her sleeve and looked up.

Mabel had the kindest eyes she had ever seen. "You did the right thing. They weren't ready to hear that they might be leaving other relatives behind, not after seeing so many murdered. They'll understand when this is all over."

Eleanor sniffed, then laughed with a sharp edge. "Really? Do you think so? Because I don't. We're starting a new world based on a lie."

Mabel crouched down beside her and spoke softly. "You did what you had to do. You're saving their lives."

Eleanor could only nod her head. She didn't believe it, but holding onto the thought was the only thing that was keeping her from spiraling.

When they were sure the tunnels were clear, Eleanor led everyone down the rock staircase and to the boats. They filled both fishing boats, there must have been at least one hundred survivors. It was dangerous making the journey on the water during the night, but they had no other choice. Thankfully the boats had large floodlights and a few of the older kids were born and raised working the fishing docks with their parents. They were a tremendous help in getting to Chesapeake Bay without incident.

Upon their arrival, they were greeted with everything they needed. Multiple vans, boxes of food, and cartons of water. Grateful to Téa for arranging everything they needed. Eleanor used their radio to check in with her niece, to tell her that they had made it to the outpost safely and were on their way to the Sanctuary. They would not be able to check in again after that as there were no more radio towers between here and their destination. The hurry in her chest wanted to leave immediately, but they spared an hour, especially for the little ones, to let everyone use the bathrooms, eat, and rest before loading into the vans and continuing their journey. Into unknown futures and the challenges that were ahead.

CHAPTER TWENTY-FIVE
Zephyr

It was the next morning and Téa had missed multiple nursing sessions. He had to give Celia formula, which he didn't mind in the slightest, but he was worried when Téa didn't come home sooner. Florence had come back to let him know that Téa was staying in the Vida Brigade radio room. That she had heard from Eleanor, but it was imperative that her aunt make it to a nearby Dunamis outpost, and Téa didn't want to miss her call. But that call was supposed to come in late last night. Téa should have been home by now.

He knew she could take care of herself, and he was trying to give her some space. But she was his world, and she was hurting. He could see it in her body, in her eyes, hear it in her voice. After making sure Celia was changed and fed, Zephyr left the baby with Emma. Then he made two thermoses of coffee and decided to go to the Vida Brigade, just to make sure she was okay.

A chill swept through the air as his steps crunched the leaves blanketing the ground. Smoke rose from chimney tops and the rising sun beamed through the branches as birds whistled their morning tunes. He was approaching the edge of the Sanctuary when he saw her moving slowly through the trees towards him.

Relief flooded him when he could see that she was in one piece. He didn't know what could have happened to her, but every worst-case scenario had plagued him with a sleepless night. He tried to shake off the tension and plastered a smile on his face so that she wouldn't see the fear that had been eating him up.

"Good morning beautiful! I thought you could use something hot this morning." He said with a wink then continued. "Emma is watching Celia, and Elijah too when he wakes up."

She laughed and that simple act brought him enormous joy.

"Did you just imply that *you* are the 'hot thing' that you were bringing me?" She laughed again.

He shrugged his shoulders. "Well, you can't say I'm wrong per se, but I suppose you'd appreciate the coffee more." He smiled and handed her the steaming beverage. "How was your night?"

She cradled the black liquid as though it were a lifeline and blew before taking a sip and replying. "Good, actually. I heard from Eleanor, and they made it safely to the outpost. They should be here early tomorrow."

She was quiet for a minute and took another drink before saying. "I'm sorry I didn't come home. I just meant to sit for a minute, and I must have fallen asleep."

Zephyr wondered if he had made her feel guilty. That was the last thing he wanted. He moved to walk closer to her as they headed back to Ian's house. "Hey, it's completely okay, and Celia's good. I'm glad you got some sleep."

They walked in silence for a moment, and he could see the tension melt off her. Finally, he felt like he could breathe again after seeing the lines between her eyes smoothen out. When she was at peace, his heart was at peace.

He pulled her gently into an embrace and kissed the top of her head. Warmth flooded him as she nuzzled under his chin, and he could feel the smile radiating throughout them both. He softly tugged her chin up and looked in her eyes. "Hey, how about we celebrate?"

Her melodic laugh sang in his ears, every moment they spent together he knew deeper and more profoundly that he would be hers for all eternity.

A tender smile tugged at her lips as she replied. "Zephyr... I hardly think this is the time to be celebrating. Now that we know we at least have a hope of succeeding, we need to make an announcement to the rest of the Sanctuary. *Florence* thought it would be best to wait and not tell everyone until we knew for sure if we'd have backup. She thought it best not to get their hopes up until we knew that we might be able to pull it off."

He loosely draped an arm around her shoulders and grinned. "Even better, we celebrate to lessen the blow. I mean, the news of impending doom is difficult to swallow. Why not throw one last hoorah?"

She laughed again. "Hoorah?"

"Yeah, you know? Shindig, hootenanny, bash, blowout, a party. Why not?"

She shook her head and those gorgeous dark curly locks swung about and glistened in the sun. "Because the world is ending tomorrow..."

He stopped and stepped in front of her. As he gently rubbed her arm, he grinned. "And there is nothing left to do but wait for help to arrive. Why sit anxiously waiting with nothing to do?"

She shook her head, not convinced. "There's plenty to do, like figuring out how to help Elijah with the dark souls for one."

"Okay, you're right about that. How about this... I can't really contribute to that particular problem. But you and Annabelle can. I'll see if Emma is willing to watch Celia. You do what you can with Elijah. And I'll make preparations for tonight."

She dug her tennis shoe into the ground and crossed her arms. "Zephyr, I just don't know that now is the best time to try and have a party. We need to conserve our resources, that's the whole reason Ian is out on a supply run."

He smiled even wider. "True, but we all have to eat anyway, right? Party decorations aren't exactly a hot commodity when starting over on a new planet. I literally have nothing to do until the others get here. Let me bring in one last bit of joy. Finding Eleanor and so many other people with abilities is a win! Let's acknowledge that."

At last, he knew he had won her over when she sighed deeply and nodded her head. He playfully squeezed her side exactly where he knew she was ticklish, and she bent over in laughter before she slyly pushed him away.

When they arrived at Ian's he checked in with Emma to see if she would be willing to watch Celia for the afternoon. She said she was happy to, that she would need the practice for when she had two little ones of her own to watch. He thanked her and did Celia's next feeding and diaper change before getting ready to leave, while Téa showered.

Zephyr was standing outside the bathroom door and when he heard the water turn off, he knocked. "It's me."

"Come in."

When he opened the door, she was wrapped in a towel and her hair was hanging in wet spirals down her back. His heart skipped a beat. *I'm so lucky.* He put his hands around her waist and pulled her close. "So, Emma is good to watch Celia and Elijah is waiting for you in the living room. Are you sure you don't need me for anything today?"

She smiled and nuzzled her nose against his. "No, you were right. There's not really much to do until Eleanor and the others get here, besides working with Elijah."

The pounding in his chest amplified and he couldn't hold back any longer. He squeezed her tight and pressed his lips against hers. She responded by parting her mouth just enough to let him know to keep going. He could feel the curve of her hips beneath the towel and she trailed her fingers down his body, leaving heat in their wake. He burned for her.

But then she pulled away gasping for breath. "Sorry, I'm still a little sore from the last time. I just barely got the okay from my obstetrician back at Sandstone during my last postpartum check-up."

He pulled back, but kept his hands on her gently and whispered. "I'd wait a lifetime for you."

The smile she gave him flamed the fire within him and he couldn't resist one last kiss. "So, I'll see you tonight?"

She grinned wider and nodded her head. He brushed her cheek softly with the back of his hand and pulled himself away. Seeing the blush on her cheeks gave him a kind of satisfaction that was unparalleled to anything he could recall.

With a spring in his step, he set off. His first stop would be the blacksmith. He wandered in the general direction of the center of the Sanctuary, hoping it would be where most of the service-type places were located. Unfortunately, Téa was the one who knew the Sanctuary well. He had scarcely explored the area, but he couldn't ask her, or anyone for directions. This had to be kept under wraps to keep it a surprise.

Finally, he turned a corner and came upon a row of what looked like small storefronts along a dirt path. He walked until he saw black smoke pouring from the top of one of the log structures more heavily than the others. When he opened the door Zephyr was in luck. This was definitely the blacksmith's shop.

It was a large open room with concrete floors and sizable rafters in the front half. A loft was up top in the back half of the shop, presumably a living space. In the middle of the room, a hot pool of lava glowed red in the center of a great stone cylinder. A burly man with a full black beard and brown skin sat next to it holding a long pair of metal tongs.

A second man wearing a heavy black leather apron, taller and thinner with fair skin and blonde hair, approached him. "Hello, can I help you?"

Zephyr cleared his throat. "Um, yes, I hope so anyway. I was wondering if you happened to make any jewelry?"

The man stared quizzically at him and tilted his head to the side before responding. "Jewelry? It's been a long time since anyone has asked about that. It's not exactly highly requested when people are just struggling to survive."

Suddenly, a hot shame flared up within Zephyr. What was he thinking? This was a stupid idea; the man was right. Of course, why would anyone ask for anything so frivolous. He shuffled awkwardly by the front door and shoved his hands in his pockets. "Right, of course, sorry to bother-"

"But, we do happen to dabble on the side, a hobby of sorts. Mostly it's my husband, Seth, who experiments here and there." He nodded to the side indicating the man who was seated by the fire.

Relief flooded through him, and Zephyr grinned. "Really? So maybe you can help me then?"

The man smiled and leaned against a counter on one side of the room with arms crossed. "Perhaps... what exactly is it that you're looking for?"

"Um…" Zephyr rubbed the back of his neck and ran his fingers through his hair. "Well, so there's this girl."

"Ah, yes, there's always a girl isn't there?" The man raised an eyebrow with a smirk on his face. He then held out his hand. "I'm Torrence."

"Zephyr, nice to meet you, Torrence."

The pair shook hands, and Zephyr's nerves began to calm.

Torrence narrowed his gaze before he asked his next question. "No offense, but I know pretty much everyone within the Sanctuary, who are you exactly?"

Zephyr laughed. "No offense taken. I'm…" He hesitated, he couldn't exactly say the General's son, considering how hated his pseudo father was, and he didn't really feel like claiming Florence as his grandmother yet. "Well, you may know my…" He hesitated again, who was Téa to him? Family, lover, baby mama, girlfriend? None of those descriptors seemed to fit. "Well, I hope she'll be my wife, Téa. You may have met her last year. She and I spent some time here. She got to know the community. I was holed up in the hospital pretty much the whole time."

Torrence's mouth dropped open and he relaxed his arms. "Holy shit! Of course, Zephyr and Téa! I can't believe I didn't pick up on that sooner. Yeah man, I know who you are." The excitement faded from Torrence and was replaced with an almost solemnity. "She saved me. Saved all of us really. We owe her our lives. Whatever you need, we'll make it happen, On the house."

Zephyr was taken aback by the mans deep reverence for Téa. He knew she had taken down the General, but they had yet to discuss the details. He tried to shake off the unsettling feeling that he still didn't know everything, but he did know one thing for sure. He loved her. With everything he had in him.

"Well, I am relieved to hear that. Thank you, Torrence." Zephyr took a deep breath and continued. "So, here's the deal. I want to propose to Téa tonight and surprise her with a wedding."

Torrence took a step back and laughed. "Woah, you sure do know how to spring something on a girl huh? And what if she says no?"

Heartbreak, despair, welcoming the end of the world.

"Then, the surprise wedding will turn into a much-needed party for the Sanctuary. A spur of the moment celebration for everything we have overcome."

Torrence's laughter continued as he shook his head. "Man, you sure do have some balls, don't you? Well, what kind of ring are you looking for? I do have to warn you, we don't exactly have access to a lot of precious gems, mostly just small accent stones, whatever we can salvage from the old mine."

Hope flowed inside of Zephyr again. He smiled wide. "Great! Actually, I plan on using her parents' wedding bands. They have a special meaning to her, but she wears them as a necklace, and I'd like to give her a new pendant to replace them."

Torrence rubbed his chin deep in thought. "Alright man, and what kind of pendant? Anything special?"

Zephyr was surprised when he felt warmth in his face. "Yea, yes, um, so the first time I told her I loved her I called her my sea star. I was hoping you could make something in the shape of a star?"

Torrence rubbed his chin in thought, and he turned away. Zephyr started to panic, was he being unreasonable?

Torrence paused and turned back around. "Well, are you coming?"

Excitement pushed Zephyr forward and he hurried to catch up. To his surprise, the bear-like man, Seth, got up and followed behind them. Torrence led the way into a small office near the back of the shop and opened the door for them all to enter. Torrence stood firmly at the entryway and Seth moved to a short desk and grabbed a wooden, hinged box.

Seth spoke for the first time, his voice surprisingly kind, but also deep and reverberating. "You are in luck, my friend. We can't exactly create a pendant from scratch by tonight. But I have been playing with these silver waxing moon pendants, and I just happen to have three of them finished."

Zephyr was quiet, he was not sure if he felt lucky. Three silver moon pendants did not scream sea star to him. But perhaps he should be grateful for anything with almost no time to prepare such a special gift.

Seth smiled expectantly, but when Zephyr didn't say anything, Seth kept talking. "You see, if you take the three moons and arrange them just so, cut one end off, sodder it back together, they form a sea star."

Seth's enthusiasm was contagious and when the man showed Zephyr how they did indeed add together to create the right shape, he was thrilled.

"That's amazing! Can you mold them together by tonight?"

Torrence's sly smile returned, and he patted Zephyr on the back. "We can do you one better than that. Not only can Seth get the pendant finished by tonight, but I will help you plan this wedding."

Zephyr chuckled. "Really? You would do that for me?"

Torrence's expression turned serious again. "You really have no idea what she did for us, do you?" Zephyr shook his head, and Torrence continued. "All you have to know, is that *everyone* will be honored to help. It will be our pleasure."

An hour before sunset, Zephyr was walking back to Ian's house. A tightly wound ball of anxious nerves. Excitement, fear of Téa saying no, and hope that she would say yes, rolled around inside him so viciously he was shaking.

Once inside he saw Téa lying on the couch, arm draped over her face as Celia napped soundly in a bassinet next to her. He tiptoed quietly to not disturb her, with a white cotton garment bag slung over his shoulder. He dropped the garment bag near the kitchen. He didn't see Elijah in the living room or kitchen and kept walking to the spare room. Zephyr knocked quietly and waited, then heard the soft clacking of Elijah's crutches before the door opened.

"Zephyr! You're back, where have you been?"

Zephyr ruffled Elijah's hair and smiled. "I have been very busy getting together an extra special surprise for Téa. But I'm not ready to talk about that yet, first I have a very important question for you."

Elijah slowly made his way over to the bed and sat down. "Okay shoot, whatcha got for me?"

Zephyr loved this kid, his genuine optimism and innocence. "Before I get to that, how did your day go with Téa? Any progress on those dark souls?"

Elijah shook his head. "No, they're all gone. Not even one was around, and I've been able to reach out to all the good souls that are attached to all the people coming here on the buses. Téa thinks the dark souls are up to something. She thinks it was too easy for them to just give up. But Annabelle is doing, re-con-no-since." Elijah smiled his toothy grin apparently very pleased with himself.

Zephyr laughed. "Do you mean, reconnaissance?"

Elijah huffed. "Yeah, that's what I said."

Zephyr chuckled. "Well, it sounds like you have it all under control. Are you ready for my very important question?"

Elijah sat up as straight as he could. "Yep, I'm ready."

Zephyr cleared his throat and took a deep breath. "I know you miss your mom and dad very much, and Téa and I would never try to take their place. But we both care about you very much, and we were wondering if you would like to officially be a part of our family?"

Elijah's face lit up in joy and he swung his short arms around Zephyr's neck hugging tightly.

Zephyr choked out a chuckle. "I'll take that as a yes."

Elijah wiped his nose and his red eyes glistened as he nodded his head.

Zephyr held back tears of his own, his nose tickled with emotion. "Are you ready for your first family assignment?"

Elijah smiled wide. "Yes!"

"I want to ask Téa to marry me tonight, do you know what that means?"

Elijah rolled his eyes. "Duh Zephyr, I'm not a baby, I'm eight and half years old."

Zephyr guffawed. "Well, if she says yes, I'd like you to be my best man. Do you think you could do that for me?"

"Yessir!" Elijah threw up his best salute.

Zephyr closed the bedroom door quietly and made his way back down the hallway. Téa was standing in the kitchen stirring a cup of tea. His heart nearly somersaulted when she smiled at him and whispered. "I didn't hear you get back. How did the party preparations go?"

He walked up behind her and wrapped his arms around her. "Perfect, they went perfectly."

She turned around in his arms and grinned. "You're happy."

He held her gaze and disappeared into her eyes. He gently took her cup and set it on the counter then pulled her into a slow twirl so that her back was against his chest, and they swayed together. He hummed a soft melody in her ear and when he felt her body relax against him, he whispered in her ear. "Marry me?"

Téa laughed, and when she turned around to see that he was serious, she smiled. "Zephyr, I would marry you every day of my life. Maybe, if we make it through this, we can have some kind of ceremony. But know this, I'm yours, always."

His happiness could no longer be contained, it bloomed inside and all around him like a living breathing thing. He held her close, his arms around her waist, and said. "Marry me, tonight."

She chuckled again, and before she could say anything he picked up the white bag that he had set down on the floor behind them. He pulled out a dress. Cream colored and decorated with the tiniest seed pearls that seemed to sparkle, long lace sleeves, and floor-length.

He delighted in her astonished gasp, and he said. "This was given to you by a woman named Mia. Apparently she makes jams and jellies for the Sanctuary. She said she was saving it for a special occasion and that our wedding would be just that."

"Oh... Zephyr, it's beautiful."

Her joy was everything to him. He held the dress out to her. "Mia said it's a relaxed fit from the waist down, and it has these pearlescent shoelace things in back to make it as tight or loose as you need."

He worried that maybe she didn't like it when she was quiet, but she said. "It's gorgeous, Zephyr. I just don't know that now is the right time—"

He heard Emma clear her throat from behind them. He turned around to see her smiling.

She said to Téa. "You hush now, this is your moment, and I would love to help you get ready. We should hurry, everyone is waiting."

Zephyr spent the next thirty minutes getting himself and Elijah dressed, and attending to Celia when she woke from her nap. And when Téa emerged from the back room, Zephyr's breath was taken straight out of his chest. She was stunning. Her hair was in a loose updo with beautiful light spirals framing her face. Her eyes were beautiful, her dress hugged her in all the right places, she was gorgeous, and she was his.

There could not possibly be a luckier man in all the world.

He passed Celia to Emma and offered his arm to Téa. She gently took it, and he opened the door. Watching her take in the sight before them was something he would never forget. The Sanctuary had outdone themselves. Even Florence pitched in.

The path in front of Ian's house was covered in wildflower petals. Twinkle lights hung in all the trees leading the way to the center of the community. Ian had arrived earlier in the day from a successful supply run and was able to get music playing. Little Nora stood next to her father holding a basket of wild feathers and small pinecones.

Zephyr didn't think he could be any more proud and grateful until they stopped at a white aisle. Hundreds of small smooth rocks had been painted white and in tiny black writing, every member of the Sanctuary had written their hopes and dreams for the future, and their well wishes for the couple.

He held Téa's hand tight and asked. "Are you ready?"

She squeezed his hand back. "Absolutely."

Chapter Twenty-Six
Téa

Téa felt like she was floating in the stars wrapped in pure bliss. She didn't know that happiness could be experienced at such a high magnitude. She would be content to never come back down to Earth. When Zephyr wrapped his arms around her during their first kiss as a married couple she melted. There was still that nagging little bit of doubt that she didn't deserve to experience such love and devotion, but she would drink it up anyway.

When Emma had walked down the aisle holding Celia in that itty bitty white dress with tiny sculpted multi-colored lace flowers, her heart spilled over. And when Elijah stood by Zephyr's side in his boy-sized suit and officially became a part of their family, she felt honored to be the parent of such a remarkable person.

Then Zephyr gently removed her parents' wedding bands from the delicate chains around her neck, placed them on each of their fingers, and put the most beautiful starfish pendant in their place. It was silver and dotted with the smallest gemstones in a variety of colors. Téa knew instantly what it signified; the first time Zephyr told her he loved her. It was perfect, and she was glowing with gratitude.

It was soul-crushing breaking the meteor news to the Sanctuary. But Zephyr was by her side, and when she could no longer speak, he spoke for them. He had a calm elegance to his demeanor. He motivated them. Encourage them to be thankful for having hope to live on, and to celebrate the blessings they had before them.

Finally, after the ceremony, when everyone was enjoying the reception Annabelle in her ghostly form whispered in Téa's ear. Téa and Zephyr had just finished their first dance, and she felt grateful, knowing that her sister was still by her side.

Annabelle whispered. "Hey Sis, *you ready to go on a trip? You still need to see our new home, or you won't be able to teleport if you can't envision where you're going.*"

Téa, who was seated at the edge of the community center taking a breather from all the dancing, nodded her head. "I'm ready." Then she laughed. "Why are you whispering though? It's not like anyone else can hear you or see you. Well, except for Elijah."

Annabelle shrugged her semi-transparent shoulders. "*I don't know, it just feels like such an important moment I didn't want to intrude.*"

The irony chuckled its way through her belly. "Really? You didn't want to intrude? Annabelle, you are never an intrusion, besides we still have a world to save." Téa's grin spread ear to ear. "Take me back to the stars sister."

Annabelle smiled. "My *pleasure*."

Téa closed her eyes, relaxed her body, and allowed her mind to connect with Annabelle through their soulmate connection. It only took a moment and in her mind's eye, they were suddenly floating in the stars. They passed galaxy after galaxy. The amazing array of hue and color against the deep blackness of space was more beautiful than anything Téa could have ever imagined.

Then, they were there. Humanity's new planet. It was more stunning than words could describe. Its magenta mountain ranges gleamed in the sun as though they were made from millions of faceted rubies. Grass that wasn't exactly grass, more purple than green and more clover than straight shoots, but nothing like Téa had ever seen on Earth. Its four moons visible even in the daytime were each larger than Earth's moon. The wildlife had more colorful plumage than any bird or animal she had ever seen. Its valleys and waterfalls were plentiful and colorful, like a rainbow after a rainstorm.

Téa was overwhelmed, at a loss for words, but filled with the desire to start over on such a beautiful planet of wonder. They had to succeed. This was the place. The home that Celia and Elijah deserved. Humanity could do it right this time.

"It's beautiful Annabelle, how did you find this place?"

Annabelle stood beside her and tilted her head in thought. *"I'm not sure. I was untethered from everything, you know, after my death. I met my sensei."*

Téa laughed. "Sensei?"

Annabelle narrowed her ghostly eyes. *"You hush, yes, I call him my sensei because he showed me the way, he has the form of a little boy, not Elijah, someone else. Anyway, I was just gliding along and then I saw the meteor, saw it headed straight for Earth. I panicked. I knew it was going to decimate everything in its path. So, I started searching, and it's like something greater than myself showed me the way."*

She laughed. *"My sensei probably pulled me towards this planet. Like a beacon in my heart. But when I tried to reach out to you on Earth, it's like your grief was pushing me away, and then I found Elijah... then, well, I had hope again."*

Suddenly a painful guttural scream pulled from somewhere deep within Téa. It bounced around her head, painfully ringing in her ears, so loud and intense it pulled her mind back to Earth. Her eyes shot open and everyone within the Sanctuary was running, and screaming.

Téa stood up from her seat and yelled. "Zephyr!" She searched frantically for her children, for her husband, and found nothing. Even Florence would have been a welcome sight, but they were gone. She started to run and tripped over something thick on the ground. She looked down and saw the empty eyes of Mia, the woman who had given the beautiful wedding dress to her.

Téa screamed out and scrambled backward on her hands, then pushed herself up and ran. The twinkle lights flickered and were hanging to the ground in some spots. The flower petals, feathers, and pinecones that little Nora had scattered across the white stone aisle were crushed and smeared like little rivers of blood. No wait, it was blood.

Whose blood is this?

Someone grabbed her arm, and she was pulled to a stop. Ian was screaming at her. "Téa! The Loyalists, they're here!"

Téa's heart pounded in her chest, she slowed her breathing and focused. The blood in her body made a whooshing sound in her ears.

"*Focus.*" Annabelle said, and she added her strength to Téa, and when she opened her eyes, she didn't see people running. She saw outlines of Sanctuary members in a cool green and Loyalists in a deep purple. As though the subconscious of her mind had memorized every community member and ingrained them in the back of her mind. Everyone else who was not remembered was an enemy.

Every purple moving figure that ran past Téa was halted, she zeroed in on its figure and pulled forth the life force from their body. Soaking in every last ounce of energy, of power from each and every intruder. She could hear nothing but their death cries as they stilled and went quiet and then dark. She didn't know how long she walked around this way, seeing nothing but green and purple, but when there was nothing except green left, she collapsed.

"Téa! Téa!"

Someone was shaking her and shouting her name. She slowly opened her eyes and could see normal again.

Ian was standing over her, panic deep within his eyes. "Are you okay?"

Téa groaned and slowly sat up. She felt as though she had two bodies. Her core body was depleted, exhausted from the physical amount of strength her abilities had used up. But there was also a second body, a shell that surrounded her. It hummed with power, barely contained, and begged to be let loose.

Her tongue thick and words heavy asked. "Ian, where's my baby? Where's Zephyr and Elijah?"

He helped her to her feet and kept his hand on her elbows to keep her steady. "They're safe. When the fighting started, he and Emma ran the kids back to the house. Zephyr didn't want to leave without you, but I forced him. I promised him I'd keep looking for you."

A rustling sound from their side made them both turn to look. It was Florence, she emerged from a set of trees. The old woman had blood dripping down her face, and she looked like she had aged. She struggled towards them and collapsed in Téa's arms.

Despite Florence's faults, Téa's empathy for the old woman outweighed any ill will she held. "Florence, what happened? Are you okay?"

Florence gasped for breath, and when she breathed deeply, she coughed up blood. Her eyes rolled and closed for a moment, then shot back open, wild, and searching.

"I didn't see them coming! They took out the Vida Brigade. I tried for two minutes to search into the future, to see a way of defeating them, but I couldn't see anything, nothing at all, it was just empty. Then one of them attacked me. I thought I was done for, but then he just dropped dead. I don't understand."

Téa's voice was solemn. "It was me. I killed all the Loyalists. That's why he dropped dead." Téa was deep in her mind, she thought back to her conversation with Louis. After they had subdued him and interrogated him in the miner's tunnel. "Louis said the loyalists needed Celia, Zephyr, and me. But why not take all three of us back at Sandstone?" She thought to herself again, and went to her conversation with Eleanor. "My Aunt said the loyalists were still experimenting. What if they didn't take us because they wanted to see our abilities in action, they needed something powerful enough to invoke a response from us, like a kidnapping."

"That means someone inside the Sanctuary was watching us, a traitor among us." Annabelle said to Téa.

Something large and loud crashed through the forest towards them. Barreling through the tree line, Seth came running towards them holding a metal rod. His eyes were completely filled in black, his mouth twisted in anger, and just as soon as he was about to take a swing, he dropped the rod and shook his head.

"What? What happened?" He cried.

Another Sanctuary member charged their group, eyes blackened and wielding a large knife. Again, just as they were about to slash out, they stopped and stood in confusion.

Téa helped Florence to her feet and swung one of the old woman's arms around Téa's shoulders. "We need to get out of here and get to the others! Something's not right."

Ian ducked under Florence's other arm and helped Téa carry her. They hurried back to Ian's house and when they burst through the front door Téa collapsed and cried tears of relief. They were safe. They were all here, Zephyr, Celia, Elijah, Emma, and little Nora.

Ian carried Florence to the couch and laid her down. Then Zephyr ran to Téa and wrapped his arms around her where she sat crying on the floor. She was safe again, warm in his arms, she clutched him tighter and let her sobs rake through her.

Someone cleared their throat and Téa looked up. It was Elijah. He was hesitant before he spoke. "Um, I think I know what's happening. I found a soul. She was a girl my age. He said the loyalists are being led by someone powerful. The bad souls, they are trying to possess us, to live again, but the human mind is too strong, it only lasts a minute or two before they get booted out."

Téa could see the struggle in Elijah's eyes. She let go of Zephyr and brought Elijah in for a gentle hug. "Hey little man, that's really helpful. You did good, are you okay?"

Elijah went limp in Téa's arms and started to cry, through a high-pitched voice he said. "That was really scary."

Téa rubbed his back in slow circles. "I know buddy, I know."

The possessions stopped, and an eerie yet determined calm spread throughout the community. Half of the Sanctuary was up all-night taking inventory of what was lost in the damage. They all knew now the importance of having the Sanctuary in top condition before the teleportation would start. Any repairs that would be needed were noted, and they started deciding which things were the most important and if they had time to run to the closest town for replacements.

They were in their final hours and the people of the Sanctuary had done as much as they possibly could to prepare. Now they just had to wait for Eleanor and the arrival of the supernaturals. Florence had said the Meteor always struck at 08:00. Eleanor and the others were due to arrive at 07:00. It was currently 06:30. They didn't have time to spare. When 07:00 rolled around, and then 07:15, Téa started to panic.

"Annabelle, can you search out Eleanor and the others?"

"*I'll try sister. It's more difficult for me to travel on Earth than in space for some reason, especially when I'm away from you and Elijah. But I'll try.*"

Téa tried to calm her nerves as she felt the connection between her and Annabelle loosen. Then she noticed her shirt was wet. She stared down quizzically, and then it hit her. Her breasts were leaking, she couldn't remember her last nursing session. The past few days were weighing heavy on Téa. She felt as though she were failing as a mother. Since Celia was born, she had spent almost every minute of every day with her baby. Now, since the kidnapping, and Emma watching Celia, and Zephyr and Celia having their soulmate connection, she felt like she wasn't holding her daughter enough.

She tried not to cry as the milk dripped down her stomach underneath her loose-fitting shirt and went to see where Zephyr and Celia had gone. It didn't take long. She found them napping in the nursery together. Celia was in the crib and Zephyr was asleep in a rocking chair. Téa soaked in their peacefulness for a moment, then slowly backed out of the room.

She was on her way to grab her breast pump when her connection to Annabelle grew stronger.

"Annabelle?"

Téa could feel the worry in her sister before Annabelle replied. "*I found them. One of the vans had a tire blowout, they're about five miles outside the Sanctuary boundary.*"

Téa hurried to the living room where she last saw Ian. She tried to keep her voice from rising as she said urgently. "Ian, we need to find a large van or a few cars. Eleanor has a flat tire some miles away. We need to go now!"

She hurried to the door with Ian on her tail when Elijah piped up from where he was sitting on the couch. "Don't worry Téa, I'll help Emma watch Nora, and I'll tell Zephyr when he wakes up."

The guilt of feeling like a failure as a mother came back strong. She hadn't even thought about Elijah before she was about to leave. She bit back the urge to cry and replied. "Thanks, little man, you're the most awesome kid ever, you know that?"

Elijah smiled wide, his grin spreading from ear to ear. "Yeah, I know."

Ian pulled on Téa's elbow. "Come on, we've got to go."

With one last glance behind her and a nod from Emma in the kitchen, Téa followed Ian out the door. They ran to the Sanctuary boundary towards the Vida Brigade. Even though the Loyalists had killed all the Vida Brigade rebels, there was not as much destruction to the outbuildings. They kept moving to where the vehicles were stored.

Most of the larger vehicles had been damaged, or the keys were missing, or tires slashed. But they were able to find two large sedans in working condition, it would have to be enough. Then they were driving, flying down the road as quickly as they could go. Téa's heart started pounding when she saw a figure walking along the side of the road. It was Eleanor.

Téa slowed down and when the car came to a stop, she jumped out of the car and raced towards her aunt. "Eleanor! Oh my God, Eleanor, are you okay?"

Ian's car was coming up behind her and she waved at him to continue going.

Then she looked at her aunt. She seemed beyond exhausted, her eyelids heavy, her walk slow but determined. And when she made eye contact with Téa, she collapsed to the ground. Téa hurried to her side and sat down next to her.

Eleanor's voice was quiet, as though her voice was dry and tired. "Yes, I'm okay. But I am sure glad to see you. We got a flat tire, maybe a mile away, not a single one of our vans had a spare tire. Without any way to contact you, I had no option but to start walking."

Téa rubbed her aunt's back, trying to comfort her. "Auntie, you have dozens of supernaturals with you, no one could find a way to get you all the rest of the distance?"

Eleanor laughed softly and dropped her head. "You don't think I thought of that?" She shook her head and continued. "One gal can fly, actually fly, can you believe that? But only for short distances and she's not strong enough to carry anyone else. Another girl can levitate objects, but nothing too heavy. Téa, we're all tired. Maybe we could have thought of a solution, but after everything we've been through and our drive here, everyone's energy is depleted."

Téa mentally kicked herself in the ass. She wasn't exactly being very comforting. The stress of running out of time was getting to her. "I'm sorry, Auntie, of course, you would have tried other solutions. If I didn't have to save my energy for teleporting an entire planet, I would have come by more efficient means, so I understand." She paused and took a deep breath. "But we need to hurry, we're down to our last thirty minutes and it'll take half of that time to get back to the Sanctuary. I'm hardly going to have any time to explain everything to the supernaturals, let alone practice with them." Téa stood and reached her hand out to help her aunt up. "Come on let's go."

When they arrived back at the Sanctuary everyone was in a frenzy. Ian shouted at Téa. "I'm going to run to the computer lab. It had a sound system that's connected to loudspeakers throughout the Sanctuary. We can make an announcement that it's time to hunker down. Everyone should stay indoors and within the Sanctuary boundaries."

Téa nodded at him as he took off. She trusted that Zephyr and Emma had the children secure, and she focused on gathering the supernaturals to explain what would happen next. They had all found out the news by word of mouth. The few kids who had heard Eleanor and Téa's conversation on the radio had told some others, and word spread. Eleanor had told Téa it was a difficult journey here. Some of the kids had demanded to go back for their remaining family. Some refused to help, some who were ready to give up and die on Earth.

But over the course of the tremendously long drive, Eleanor, with the help of Mabel was able to inspire hope in them. They were all on board with helping by the time they arrived, even if a few were still reluctant, or had simply given up fighting, resigned to whatever fate that was to come.

There were very few members of the Sanctuary that had abilities. But Ian and Emma did, being soulmate couples. Their powers, however, had yet to make themselves known, plus she didn't want to put a very pregnant Emma at risk. Then there was Zephyr and Celia with their recently discovered soulmate powers, plus Celia's abilities that she was born with. But Téa refused to include Celia in the chain connection or to make orphans of their children. And if the teleportation worked, but the supernatural's didn't make it, then she at least needed Zephyr to survive for them.

This left nine supernaturals from the Sanctuary, plus the people that Eleanor had brought. Téa hoped it would be enough.

As they formed a wide circle in the center of the Sanctuary, Téa shouted to them. "Hold hands with the person next to you." Her heart raced, her legs shook, and she worried they would see the fear and apprehension written all over her face. "A young boy has the ability to speak to your loved ones who have passed on. Some of you may be able to see or hear your loved one, others may not, but they are here with us." Téa took a deep breath and looked at the watch on her wrist, five minutes until impact.

Téa gripped Florence's hand tight. The old woman insisted on helping, but she could hardly stand. Florence nodded at Téa to continue.

Téa took a deep breath and let it out slowly. "I want you all to tap into your powers in your mind and feel for a tether. Your loved ones are going to link you into a powerful force of energy. Once we are all connected, I will enclose the entire Sanctuary in a translucent bubble, five miles deep into the Earth and five miles tall into the sky, like a giantterrarium, then I will harden that bubble. We will all be mentally and powerfully joined to one another, during this time I will show you mental images of our new planet. We will all focus on that destination. With our combined force, I will teleport us home. Do you all understand?"

The large group all nodded in unison. Téa could sense the tension surrounding them. The terror they all must be feeling. She looked at her watch, three minutes. They needed to start this, *now*.

Téa reached for Annabelle, and when she felt her sister's spirit she smiled.

"*You ready sister?*"

"Ready as I can be."

With one last shaky breath, Téa shouted to the group. "Now!"

The build-up of energy was instantaneous. Téa closed her eyes, and she could see everyone in the circle floating on another plane of existence. All hands joined together and focusing all their might on the task at hand. The energy field was growing bigger and stronger until it shot out and encircled the outside of the entire Sanctuary. A light, like a fireball, started spinning around them, faster and faster. This was working, it was going to work. The sounds of the world were drowned out, and all she could see was the ring of flowing fire. All she could hear was the crackling of energy, sparking, igniting, and swirling together to add to the strength of the ring.

Téa focused her mind on the new planet. On its array of color and wonder. She could feel everyone, see the image she had projected into their minds. And when they all started to think only of their new home, the power of their connection grew.

Suddenly the light began to dim. The ring of fire was slowing, and blackness was creeping in. Annabelle screamed in Téa's mind. "*They're here! The dark souls! Oh my God Téa, it's the General! He's leading them!*"

No. This can't be happening, not now. Téa screamed and tightened her grip on the hands on either side of her. "Focus! FIGHT BACK! FOCUS ON PUSHING THEM OUT!"

Téa grunted and yelled from the effort, her body was being drained, they were so close. Then she heard Florence whisper next to her. "Take my life force Téa. Take every last drop and get us home."

Téa was crumbling from the pressure, the pain of stretching herself so thin. "I can't Florence, I can't kill you."

The old woman whispered again. "I'll be dead soon anyway. Take it Téa, take it now before it's too late."

Tears rolled down Téa's cheeks, as stabbing pains shot through her heart. She screamed and searched for Florence's life force, and in taking the old woman's energy, she accessed all the rest. All the Loyalists she had murdered, their energy was still sitting outside herself, humming with power. She tapped into the electricity that was begging to be set free and the ring of light exploded. Téa focused on the new planet, the power was too much to rein in, too strong.

Téa screamed out for Annabelle. "Help me!!"

Téa could feel Annabelle reaching, her ghostly fingers outstretched, searching for each other. Annabelle pushed harder at the Generals' evil soul trying to engulf her and reached again for Téa. When the two sisters connected, one final blast of energy shot out, and the ring of fire engulfed them all.

Then, nothing but darkness.

When Téa opened her eyes, she was lying flat on her back. She looked to the sky and saw not one, but four moons. The grass underneath her palms wasn't scratchy, or poky, but soft like silk.

Am I dead?

"No, *sister.*" Téa heard Annabelle laugh in delight. "*You're not dead at all, you did it! You teleported the Sanctuary home.*"

"But the bad souls, the fire?"

"*The final blast pushed all the dark shadows away. And in that last split second before you passed out, you succeeded!*"

Téa looked up and saw her sister's ghost dancing above her, clapping her hands in delight. Téa looked to her side, and her heart dropped at the sight of Florence's dead body. The old woman gave her the final push she needed to survive.

"*Well, glad I finally got your approval. I only had to die huh?*" Florence's ghost scoffed.

Téa sat up fast in surprise, her vision swimming from the sudden movement. "Florence?"

"*Yeah, it's me. Listen, dear, the Generals' soul and his loyalist shadows hitched a ride here. Me and the good guys have been trying to keep them away, but it seems they can't inhabit human bodies on this planet, not even for a moment. But you're going to have to look out for the animals. Especially the beasts.*"

"Beasts? What the fuck do you mean beasts!"

Téa's pulse raced. She had survived the impossible only to be thrust headfirst into a new challenge. Just as she was struggling to her feet, Zephyr who was holding Celia, and Elijah, came hurrying towards her.

Zephyr hugged her closely and kissed her intently before he released her and said. "Thank God you're okay."

Téa looked around her. The other supernaturals were all still unconscious in a circle on the ground around her, but they were alive and rousing. She looked past them and gasped. The Sanctuary had made it. Not just the inhabitants, but the structures, everything just as they had planned.

She looked at her family, Zephyr, Celia, and Elijah, and she knew there were dangers still lurking and waiting for their moment to strike. But for now, they were safe.

They were together.

They were home.

Stay Tuned...

THE BONE INVENTORY, a Stars Like Acid prequel is coming September 18th 2024.

And the epic conclusion to the Stars Like Acid series, STARS RAIN DOWN, is coming March 18th 2025

About the Author

Marissa, Latina (she/her) of mixed heritage, has always found her safe place in the world of stories. Now, she's creating her own worlds in the scope of speculative fiction, and hopes to provide the same joy to her readers.

She spent many years volunteering with children in foster care and group homes which greatly influenced her writing.

Beyond writing, Marissa enjoys anything artsy and creative, like making jewelry, painting, and photography.

She currently lives in the Rocky Mountains of western Colorado with her family, connecting with the soul of the Earth through the appreciation of nature.

STARS LIKE FIRE is her second novel.